GODOLPHIN ARABIAN.

To the RIGHT HON.ble LORD FILES OF GODOLPHIN OSBORNE &c. This is Respectfully Inscribed by the PROPRIETORS.

THE
GODOLPHIN
ARABIAN

Eugene Sue
Translated and Adapted
by Alex de Jonge

THE DERRYDALE PRESS

LANHAM AND NEW YORK

THE DERRYDALE PRESS

Published in the United States of America
by The Derrydale Press
A wholly owned subsidiary of
The Rowman & Littlefield Publishing Group, Inc.
4501 Forbes Boulevard, Suite 200, Lanham, Maryland 20706

Distributed by NATIONAL BOOK NETWORK, INC.

First Derrydale Printing 2004
Translation Copyright © 2004 by Alex de Jonge

Libarary of Congress Cataloguing-in-Publication Data
Sue, Eugene, 1804–1857.
[Arabian Godolphin. English]
The Godolphin Arabian / Eugene Sue ; translated and
adapted by Alex de Jonge.
p. cm.
ISBN 1-58667-102-2 (hardcover : alk. paper)
I. De Jonge, Alex, 1939– II. Title.
PQ2446 .A8913 2003
843'.7—dc21
2003012614

♾™ The paper used in this publication meets the
minimum requirements of American National Standard
for Information Sciences—Permanence of Paper for
Printed Library Materials, ANSI/NISO Z39.48–1992.
Manufactured in the United States of America.

Contents

v

Contents

Introduction

There is something about the outside of a horse that is good for the inside of a man.

—attributed to Sir Winston Churchill

EUGENE SUE'S *The Godolphin Arabian* begins as fiction and ends as history. Sue's tale of how a colt foaled in Yemen became one of the foundation stallions of the English Thoroughbred breed is well enough told to delight any horse lover who enjoys a story. But like all good fiction it also has its own kind of truth. We learn how reluctant English breeders were to recognize the remarkable quality of Arab bloodstock. More important, we are reminded of the extraordinary nature of the bond between an Arab and his horse, a bond that approaches veneration. It is not for nothing that Arabs describe the eye of their horse as "The Eye of Allah." Even now, anyone who has owned an Arab will know that traces of that breed's capacity for intense one-person loyalty persist to this day.

For *The Godolphin Arabian* is not just the story of a horse; it is also a story of love, loyalty, and an unswerving trust in destiny. Agba, the Godolphin Arabian's faithful companion, may be an invention—unlike his other companion the tabby cat, Grimalkin—but Sue's depiction of the glorious relationship between man and horse projects a higher truth that transcends mere fiction. This is why it is so appropriate that it should have been Agba's sole act of courageous disobedience that gave the stallion his place in history.

The author of the story, Eugene Sue (1804–1857), was a man of parts. He is best known today as one of France's first writers of serialized best-sellers, books with titles like *The Wandering Jew* and *The Mysteries of Paris*. He was a celebrity in his day, renowned for his dandyish appearance and the elegance of his turnout. Yet at the same time he was a socialist member of the Chamber of Deputies. He was also a horse lover and a founding member of the French Jockey Club, which was established with the express aim of improving French bloodstock until it could compete on level terms with its British rivals. Tragically he did not live to see the day that the French colt Gladiateur won the Epsom Derby. Lovers of English racing who remember the incomparable Mill Reef (a direct descendant of the Godolphin Arabian) and his victory in the Prix de l'Arc de Triomphe will probably understand what Frenchmen felt that day.

Of the two other translations of Sue's book, one is archaic and the other is in verse—which is why the time seemed ripe for a third. I tried to avoid archaism and Victorian slang, without lapsing into twenty-first century anachronisms. I also made some minor factual adjustments to Sue's text. The stallion's white mark was on his off hind, not his near. Eclipse died in 1789, not 1798. One of his progeny was named Babraham, not Babram. It is understandable enough that Sue should have made a few factual errors, since he did not have the magnificent resources of the National Sporting Library in Middleburg, Virginia, at his disposal, let alone the equestrian expertise of Margo Corddry; Dr. Helen Poland, DUM; and Carron Smith-Hernadez. This translation would not have been possible without them.

Chapter One

The Quaker

THE WINTER OF 1732 had been a hard one with many frosts. Toward the end of that January a good-sized crowd had gathered by the Pont-Neuf where the Rue Dauphine met the Quai des Augustins.

Nothing was or, alas, remains more common than the sad sight that had drawn these idle spectators. The roadway, made slippery by the frost, provided no traction for horses, particularly one, seen harnessed to a great cart loaded with lumber.

Chapter One

At that moment a man came by and paused to see what the crowd was about. Of medium height, middle-aged, and a trifle portly, he wore an old grey overcoat and a flat three-cornered hat that barely covered his head with its unpowdered grey hair. He wore a thick cambric cravat whose ends crossed his coat like a priest's bands and his face radiated gentle good humor. But the moment he saw the carter brutally thrust his burning torch at the horse, his expression changed to one of horror and anguished pity. Unable to tolerate the spectacle any longer he stepped forward and boldly tugged at the carter's smock.

The other onlookers were moved by a blend of curiosity and apprehension at the stranger's rashness, since his age and his gentle appearance contrasted sharply with the strapping size and raging fury of the horse's owner. The Quaker—for the man in question was indeed a member of

that sect, which entertains the most generous and compassionate feeling toward
animals—went up and took quite a strong
hold of the carter's arm. The carter turned
around at once with a threatening gesture
and asked, waving his torch, "Who grabbed
my arm just now? You, was it?"

"My friend," the Quaker replied
calmly and softly as he showed the carter
the fifteen gold pieces he held in his
hand, "Will you sell me that horse for fifteen gold pieces?"

"What!" replied the carter, taking the
offer for a bad joke.

"I'm offering you fifteen gold pieces
for your horse. Will you sell him to me?"

"You want to buy my horse for fifteen
pieces of gold, fifteen Louis d'or?" the
carter asked incredulously. He put the
torch out by treading on it with a massive foot and stared at the money in the
Quaker's hand with an expression that
blended greed and suspicious disbelief.

"Fifteen Louis, my friend," the Quaker replied with calm confidence.

"And why the devil would you want to buy my horse?"

"No matter why. Will you sell him to me?"

The onlookers were beginning to get interested, scarcely appreciating the compassionate motive of the Quaker who felt obliged to rescue one of God's creatures from such cruel treatment. There was, moreover, a second reason that we will reveal in due course that helped fuel his generosity.

"But what will you do with the horse without the cart?" the carter inquired.

"If you sell me the horse, my friend, you'll unload the cart, unharness this poor creature, gently help him up, and take us both to his stable where I'll tell you what to do next."

"What about the cart and the timber?"

"Someone will keep an eye on them until you can find another horse, and if needs be I'll cover the cost."

"Fifteen pieces of gold," replied the carter, who could not believe his luck. "And are they real?"

"Pick any coin, my friend, take it to a merchant and ask him if it is real."

The carter took his advice and came back radiant.

"Shake on it. The deal is done, good sir. You won't back out now will you?"

"Certainly not," said the Quaker. "But now, my friend, help me unharness this poor animal you've sent to his knees with the weight of the cart."

"Now that the deal is done, m'sieu, why the devil did you pay so much for a brute like this? For I don't suppose you know it, but he's a real brute, this horse is."

"I can tell you now my friend, I bought this poor creature to save it from your wickedness."

Chapter One

The carter stared at the Quaker in amazement, gave a shrug, and took another look at the gold. Finding such compassion beyond his understanding and convinced he was dealing with a madman, he started to unharness the horse.

Although by and large the spectators agreed with the carter, they did their best to help the Quaker unload the cart and free the horse. The poor creature was bleeding all over; the heavy harness and the shafts of the cart had rubbed him raw in many places and he was so terrified that the carter's slightest movement made him recoil, quiver, or shy away as if he expected another beating at any moment.

"Now, my friend, let's take the horse back to his stable," said the Quaker.

Followed by a handful of spectators, the carter, the Quaker, and the horse set off down the quay.

Chapter Two

The Tale

WE SAID THAT the Quaker had a special reason for taking pity on the horse and saving it from its cruel master. Just that morning he had received letters from London telling him that his dearest wish had been granted and his daughter had born a son. Wishing, as it were, to thank heaven for the news, the Quaker felt he could do no better than perform such an act of kindness.

He walked behind the carter, and from time to time he patted the horse's wretched, scrawny neck, contemplating the creature he had saved from such a cruel fate with an air of gentle satisfaction.

"You, m'sieu, look like a decent sort," said the carter, "And I don't want to pull the wool over your eyes. Now that the deal is done I can honestly tell you that the horse you've bought isn't just an ordinary brute. He's the vilest animal in the world, so bad tempered, crooked, and mean that he saw the end of my stick more often than he saw his nose bag. It got so bad, there were times I only dared feed him off the blade of my shovel."

"Was he like that when you bought him, or did you make him like that?"

"Well you see, he started to play games with me. I bought him cheap for twenty ecus, which was nothing, right? So I put him between the shafts. If the cart was lightly loaded, or the brute was still trying, it went off all right. But with a heavy load like this one, he'd start to act up. He'd only pretend to pull against the collar, so I'd start to whip him—whip him hard the way you saw. But you'll soon find out what a sly rascal he is. At the beginning, he used to pretend to put up with the whipping and not try to get his own back, but in the end, m'sieu, do you know, the filthy beast began to hold his whippings against me. He'd try and kick me as I was putting his harness on or off. Well, I can tell you, I soon found a way to stop him playing that game, didn't I?"

"How my friend?"

"I never did take it off!"

"How did he lie down?"

"He never did."

"Never, day or night?"

"Neither day nor night. I put him away in my barn between the shafts. He'd spend the night there standing up and spend the day getting the stiffness out of his legs by working for me."

"Do you mean to say that you never let the wretched animal sleep?"

"Him? He was far too crafty and far too tired not to sleep. He was used to sleeping on his feet wasn't he? Besides, just in case he decided to fall ill sooner or later, I let the blackamoor unharness him on Sundays, which turned Sundays into a real holiday for the blackamoor and the horse and the cat."

"What are you talking about my friend?"

"Why then, m'sieu it's a whole story, isn't it, and it tells you that people are a lot more stupid and more wild than animals are. Fair enough for the cat. It's what cats do, isn't it. But the blackamoor is bloody incredible."

"I don't understand, my friend."

"Well, it's like this, m'sieu. I've got this cat, see—an alley cat as ugly as sin.

Would you believe it, it's fallen for this nag of mine."

"For your horse?"

"Right. Would you believe it, a cat falling for a horse? I can understand the blackamoor being head over heels for it. I mean, he's a fellow, isn't he, and they come from the same parts. But a cat? But you'll see for yourself. Soon as the nag gets home, the cat jumps on the cart and onto his back, purring like a bloody drum roll. And would you believe it, the nag seems to recognize him. He nickers as if he's calling him and that bloody cat turns up immediate, jumps on the feed bin, and that stupid horse starts nuzzling and grooming him. You'll see for yourself, m'sieu. I swear it's better than a circus act. You could earn a living putting on the cat, the horse, and the blackamoor."

The good Quaker had every reason to be amazed by the singular affection displayed by a horse for a cat, but since this is how it really was there is no getting away from it.[1]

"Where did you buy the horse?" he asked the carter.

"From one of the king's cooks. Because, believe it or not, the nag comes from the king's stable."

An astonished Quaker gave the carter a long, hard look and then turned to the horse, but could see nothing about it that spoke to its royal origins. Accordingly he asked the carter to tell him how he came to be the owner of the horse.

"Oh it's a simple enough story. This horse used to belong to the king and he was used to pull the kitchen carts that run between Paris and Versailles. But he was such a brute, so difficult with other

---

1. The author wants his readers to understand that the cat is no invention. He really existed and a close emotional bond existed between him and the horse until their dying days.

horses. Kept trying to cover the mares, he did, because, begging your pardon, the beast's entire isn't he, that no one could do anything with him. So one day the head man in the kitchen decided the horse had to go, but he couldn't find a buyer because people knew too much about him to lay out good money. So he was given to one of the undercooks who thought he knew horses and could manage the nag. But what happened? One fine day the horse sunk his teeth into him and took out a great piece of his behind, breeches and all, he did. That was it for the cook, and one of his minions told me I could have him for thirty crowns. So I offered twenty, didn't I, and 'Sold!' he said. So I thought you were joking when you offered fifteen pieces of gold."

"But do you know where the horse came from before he was in the king's stables?"

"I know he come from foreign parts, a long way away. The blackamoor knows where."

"Who exactly is this blackamoor you keep talking about?"

"He's a beggar, isn't he? Poor bugger with a face the color of mahogany, comes from the same place the horse did. Someone in the kitchens told me that the nag, along with a bunch of others, was sent to the king as a present by the king of the Blackamoors. Trouble is they turned out to be a sorry lot, not worth the oats they fed them. So they sent most of them to pull the garden carts where they soon died off and I ended up with this one here."

Bearing in mind that the horse came from foreign parts and had been a gift to the King of France, the Quaker took another look at his purchase. Although no expert, he had seen plenty of horses in his day and still couldn't understand why it should have been a royal present.

Putting his bewilderment aside, he sought to learn more about the bond between the horse and the fellow the carter referred to as the blackamoor.

"So tell me more about this man who I understand comes from Africa, and whom you call 'the blackamoor.'"

"He got here with some other fellows who came with the horses and who all looked as if their faces had been carved out of mahogany. But for some reason he stayed behind in Versailles when they left. They let him lodge at the royal stables as long as the horse was there, but when it came to me he followed it and now he hangs around here and begs for a living."

"He must be really fond of it then?"

"Fond! Fond isn't the word. They're inseparable and one as lazy as the other. Bloody man. Besides, the blackamoor— African to you, m'sieu—tried to tell me, pulling faces and waving his hands—he's dumb you see, dumb as the horse with about that much tongue left—tried to tell me, he did, he'd groom the horse for nothing. Groom him, right! Start grooming a horse and you'll make him soft as a woman. Nobody grooms me, right? Why should he be groomed?"

"But my friend, you at least allowed this unhappy creature to see the horse as much as he wanted?"

"Well I thought about it, didn't I, because it was him who was putting the horse up to his tricks and made him so vicious and all. But I used to laugh when I saw them together so I let him stay. They were something to look at, I can tell you.

"Soon as I went out, the blackamoor, who'd spent the night sleeping beside the horse, would go out to beg. But by the time I'd get back, he'd be there again, waiting for his horse; and the cat was, too. If I'd decide to keep the wretched quad in his harness, he'd stay there for hours, squatting on his haunches like an ape, and he'd never take his eyes off the horse. Go to sleep like that he would. But if I wanted to see him get up to his tricks, all I had to do was let him unharness the beast and take him some feed. Which I sometimes did Sundays. And then, m'sieu, you'd die laughing. He'd come and go, round and round the horse, kiss him and stroke him, take his head in his hands, get on him, and get down again. Then, although I told him not to, he'd try to groom him, get the mud off of him, rub his old eyes with his hand. Then if he had sore places—and he always did, because a sore place is better than spurs to make him hark to me— then the blackamoor would stare at them for hours like his heart was breaking. Then one night I caught him; he was blowing on a sore place the brute had on his head! I tell you, m'sieu, I've got a little daughter, but I don't suppose I love her half as much as what he loves his horse."

"And it looks as if the horse loves him back," said the Quaker who was moved almost to tears at the story of their mutual attachment.

"Doesn't it? It's all even funnier than the cat, who seems attached to them both. Soon as the horse sees him—the blackamoor that is—he whinnies at him, lays back his ears, and scrapes his foot. If he's in harness, that is. But if I let him be unharnessed and turned loose, that's when the real fun begins. The nag lies down, gets up, stretches his head out, and makes a strange sound; and the cat and the blackamoor seem to listen, and it's hard to say which one of them looks sillier."

"And weren't you moved by the sight?"

"Moved, was I? Moved to near die laughing, I was. But then one day something really funny happened. I was giving the horse a good whipping when all of a sudden the blackamoor lost his temper and tried to hit me. But hold on, m'sieu, you can see that when you've got fists like these (the carter showed him what he was talking about) you've no call to be afraid of a blackamoor thin as a reed. So after I beat him up to teach him to mind his own business, I started whipping the horse again. Then, would you believe it, the blackamoor started to weep—he what hadn't shed a tear when I was thumping him. Now he went down on his bloody knees and showed me his back, asked me to beat him instead of the nag. How stupid can he be, m'sieu, right?"

When he heard the brute talk so crudely about the bond between these two companions in misfortune, the Quaker became really upset and was more pleased than ever that his spur of the moment purchase would reunite the man and the horse that a strange destiny had brought to France in circumstances that we shall now recount.

Chapter Three

El Scham and Agba

THE CARTER was telling the truth; the horse that he had put between the shafts of his wretched, overloaded conveyance had been one of eight horses known as "barbs" that the Dey of Tunis had presented to Louis XV in 1731, in recognition of a trade treaty that he had struck with Viscount de Manty, commander of the royal fleet, acting in the name of the French king.

After briefly attracting the attention, or rather the curiosity, of the king and his court, these eight barbs, with their rapid, forward gaits, their wild manners, their skin and bone appearance that had been compounded by the rigours of their journey, were at first accorded the most casual of receptions at the royal stables and were subsequently the objects of a scornful and neglectful dismissal.

The explanation for their rejection was simple. When it came to war or the hunt, the king favoured a breed of English horse, raised in the county of Suffolk—short loined, well ribbed up, and going close to the ground—the kind known in France as "courtauds" or crops. Since fashion was dictated by the royal taste, it is understandable that a derisive reception was accorded the barbs, with their thin necks and flat shoulders, their projecting bones, and their lean and sinewy frames—all characteristics of that precious breed whose purity had been conserved with a scrupulous care that was tantamount to veneration in the deserts of Arabia.

Of the eight Arab grooms that the Dey had sent across to accompany the horses, Agba the Mute—the one the carter called the blackamoor—alone chose to remain in France rather than return to Tunis. He had concealed himself in order not to be separated from his charge, the stallion El Scham, which he had raised and which he loved like only Arabs love their horses— that is to say with total passion. Besides, a second and most peculiar reason helped account for his attachment, one which is almost certainly without precedent.

It would appear that someone working in the royal stables had taken an interest in the mute and done what he could to help him, permitting him to remain there and providing him with food and lodging. As long as El Scham was a part of the royal household, the grooms were all too happy to let Agba take care of the barb, but once he was sold on and fell into the hands of the carter, the mute followed him and shared his miserable lot.

And yet this horse, so despised in France to the great mortification of Agba, was one of the most worthy descendants of one of the greatest bloodlines of Barbary—horses known, because of their extraordinary strength, speed, and stamina, as the Kings of the Wind.

The Dey believed he was presenting the King with a magnificent and royal gift when he sent him El Scham. As was the custom, he travelled with the record of his long and illustrious pedigree on a scroll that was kept in a little camel hair sachet, richly embroidered, which hung from his neck by a silk cord of red and gold. But when he entered the royal stables the ignorant grooms threw away the precious sachet, together with various magic amulets designed to bring the horse good luck.

Appalled by such an act of ignorant sacrilege, one which made him fear the worst for El Scham, Agba had carefully retrieved and preserved these objects in the hope of one day adorning his horse with them again, the better to guard him against the innumerable misfortunes that, he could see, had already begun to threaten his charge and that a despairing Agba attributed in great measure to the loss of these amulets.

His love of the horse is easy to understand. He had lived all his life at the Dey's stud. He had been present at El Scham's birth and watched him develop his extraordinary qualities as he grew up. But what had been and remained the subject of a quite extraordinary attention on the part of Agba (a blend of hope and of apprehension) was the fact that the horse combined two remarkable and fateful portents—one good, the other bad—portents that, according to local superstition, would exert the most extraordinary influence upon El Scham's future.

Chapter Three

It may or may not be widely known that Arabs and Berbers who know their horses recognize seventy signs of good and ill fortune that they use to cast horoscopes for their animals. Now it so happened that El Scham possessed two signs of an extraordinary power—one the portent of a wretched existence, the other predicting glory. The first, formed by a strange whorl in his coat, had the form of a wheatear, a marking considered to be one of the unluckiest signs a horse could ever have. The second sign, portent of a long life and illustrious future for the horse and his countless offspring, was a little white mark that El Scham, who was a dark bay, displayed on his off hind coronet.

Constantly torn between promises of good fortune and disaster ever since leaving Tunis, Agba had suffered a series of ups and downs, moments of hope alternating with moments of despair.

El Scham had initially been a gift to a king of France, one of the most powerful monarchs in the world, and in this Agba saw the work of the white mark. But all too soon, El Scham was ejected from the royal stable to become a draft horse, standing between the shafts of a timber merchant's cart. Agba could only ascribe such a fall to the influence of the wheatear, the fall aggravated further still by the loss of the lucky charms that Agba dared not restore to the barb for fear of provoking yet another act of brutal sacrilege from the timber merchant.

Perplexed as he was, Agba sometimes yielded to bouts of bitter despair; but at other times, in a less somber mood, he refused to abandon hope. He viewed El Scham's current dangerous condition as a time of trial, and with the Arab's faith in the incontrovertible value of signs and portents, he took comfort and deepened his understanding of the reasons for his extraordinary attachment to the horse. Had El Scham been destined to be completely happy or completely miserable, he would have submitted to the will of Allah. Unable to help him in any way, he would have stood by and watched fate take its course. But the two opposing signs of misery and triumph suggested that the stallion was destined to undergo innumerable ups and downs from which he might finally emerge to win fame and glory. Since El Scham's fate remained uncertain, Agba felt that he must never cease to share it with him. It was not Allah's will that El Scham should always be unhappy, or else Allah would not have given him a white mark on his off hind coronet, nor did He want him always to live in glory, for He had also placed the mark of the wheatear upon him. Allah is great and His will is His will.

But, despite this readiness to abandon himself to the will of Allah, as Agba saw

El Scham go down and down in the world to the point that he found himself between the shafts of the timber merchant's cart, there were times when he was tempted to abandon all hope. At those moments he was prone to believe that the period of good fortune promised by the white stocking had run its course and that from now on the wheatear would alone regulate El Scham's existence.

Indeed before journeying to France, what more could have been added to the glorious destiny that the fates had promised him? The proud descendant of a long line of famous ancestors, had El Scham not been one of the Dey's favourites? He had taken oats from his master's hand and often drunk mare's milk from a white marble trough. Proudly he had gone through his paces with saddle cloths of tiger skin or angora wool, shaking the silken crest of his gold and purple bridle and playing with his steel bit chastened with silver. Countless times he had galloped his way to victory in the desert races, while his suppleness, grace, and balance had brought triumph after triumph at the Dey's war games. As kind and obedient as he was fiery and brave, at night, when the caravan was resting in an oasis and the night burned with a myriad stars, he would enter the green and red tent to lick the hand of his sleeping master. Finally he had ruled like a sultan over a harem of the finest and proudest of his master's mares, destined as he was to perpetuate the illustrious purebred race of the Kings of the Wind.

What new happiness could the poor barb hope for in this cold and accursed land of France?

But let us return to the carter and the Englishman who were about to arrive at the stable where they would find the mute and El Scham's faithful cat.

Chapter Four

The Man, the Horse, and the Cat

THE CARTER LIVED in a kind of hovel on the Rue Guénégaud—a dark, airless yard, surrounded by high walls, with a stagnant, greenish well and a long shed with a canvas awning for a roof where Agba lived. Seeing that he was at home the carter drew him to the Quaker's attention.

"Look m'sieu, there he is. I knew he and the cat would be waiting for me."

The Quaker noticed Agba immediately. He was so wrapped in thought he had not heard them arrive. The Arab seemed to be about thirty years old. He was short,

thin, and wiry. His dark face radiated sen-
sitivity, gentleness, and a remarkable
intelligence; his nose was straight and el-
egant, his black beard was fine and curly,
he had prominent cheekbones and hollow
cheeks. He sported a small turban that
once had been white. Squatting on his
heels, he was almost completely en-
veloped in a hooded burnous of coarse,
black camel hair. Despite the cold, his feet
were bare. He was cuddling a grey tabby
cat that started at the sound of the new
arrivals. Its sudden movement aroused
the Arab who looked up anxiously. But as
soon as he heard the clink of the harness
and the horse's footsteps, he got up and
went to the courtyard entrance as if to
discover the reason for their untimely return.

He was amazed not only to see that El
Scham had been freed from his cart but
that his master actually appeared to be
treating him with a measure of kindness.

As for the cat, it jumped straight onto the horse's back, but for once El Scham appeared to ignore his friend's attentions, as if he too were amazed at the alteration in his master's behavior.

The Arab was worried, he looked from the horse to the carter to the Quaker, but when he noticed the latter's kindly expression and the way he was patting El Scham, Agba could not suppress a glimmer of hope, thinking that perhaps the streak of ill fortune had run its course.

Nothing could be more moving than the expression of restrained care and concern with which the mute proceeded to look El Scham over. But all of a sudden he knelt down, wrung his hands in desperation, and shot a fleeting, but hate-filled, glance at the carter.

He had just noticed that El Scham had terrible scarred knees caused by his two falls. Seeing these two open wounds, the Arab sunk his head in anguish and let his arms dangle loosely at his sides. To see his beloved El Scham with scarred knees was the ultimate in disgrace and degradation.

Unable to bear this spectacle of misery a moment longer, the Quaker anticipated with pleasure the Arab's reaction to the good news he was about to hear.

"Does he understand French?" He asked the carter.

"Very nicely, m'sieu. He's not always as stupid as he looks."

"My friend," the Quaker said to the mute as kindly and gently as he could, "Would you please untack the horse, groom him, and give him his feed."

The Arab was so intent on inspecting the damage done to the horse that the Englishman had to repeat himself and give him a tap on the shoulder to attract his attention.

When he finally heard him, Agba gave a sad shake of his head. Bowing to him tearfully he indicated the carter with a glance that combined fear and scarcely repressed rage.

"Go on then, you can coddle your nag all you want," said the brute. "He's not mine any more is he? He belongs to m'sieu now." And, turning to the Quaker, "Now then, I've got to find another horse haven't I? Pleasure to do business with you and good luck. If you don't have a stable you can borrow mine for the time being."

He bade the Quaker a final farewell and went away.

At first the Arab seemed not to have understood the carter, but when he saw him leave and heard the same story from the strange visitor himself, he went to his knees and kissed the hem of his coat with an expression of the utmost respect. In his rapture he even made a few muted inarticulate sounds, the extent of the poor man's expressive ability.

"Please get up my friend, please get up," said the Quaker. "Man should kneel to God alone. Now set to and do what you can for the horse. He is mine now and you will never leave him if you are willing to follow and serve me faithfully."

So overcome with joy was Agba when he heard these words that he went once more to his knees before the Quaker whose right foot he placed upon his forehead, thereby making it clear to his new master that he was making a sacred pledge to render him true and faithful service for the rest of his life.

"That will do, that will do," said the Quaker. "I will say again that no man should ever kneel before his like. Be honest and true and you will more than repay me. Now look after the poor beast. He needs your help sorely for he has suffered more than enough."

Agba slipped out of his burnous, baring his thin sinewy arms, and went up to

El Scham, contemplating him for a moment with an expression of profound—almost possessive—delight. Then, in a kind of frenzy, he started to free him from his crude harness. In an instant he had taken off the heavy collar with its sheepskin cover; the heavy, painted, brass-studded saddle; the rawhide bridle; and the rusty iron bit; and cast them all scornfully to one side. He then took out a kind of fingerless hair glove that he used to start grooming El Scham in the Tunisian style that never uses a curry comb that would soon damage the fine, silken coat of a purebred Arabian.

Now that the stallion was free of his harness, his new owner could examine El Scham more closely.

He was a very dark bay, standing about fifteen hands with a small white mark on his off hind coronet. He was terrifyingly thin. His bones seemed to be sticking through his skin that was so fine and delicate that it had been scarred all over by the heavy collar and the iron-bound shafts of the cart. The dust and dirt that covered the unfortunate beast made his coat, which had once gleamed, seem dull and ill-conditioned. The mane was tangled, dusty, and unkempt. And yet, anyone with an eye for a horse would have overlooked his wretched condition and concentrated upon El Scham's remarkable conformation. His deep chest, the sign of unusual lung capacity, would have told him that he had stamina and speed. He would have been confirmed in that opinion by the straightness and strength of his legs, so well proportioned that attention would have been quite distracted from the terrible wounds on his knees. Above all, his great hocks seemed to be the steel springs of those iron legs, for it was first and foremost their extraordinary quality that marked El Scham as a worthy descendant of the Kings of the Wind.

Yet nothing in the world is completely perfect. The kind of compulsive critic who is always prompt to find the flaw in a diamond or a wrinkle on the face of a beautiful woman would probably have noted that, despite the matchless lightness of his neck and wither, there was something a little awkward about the set of El Scham's head, which was also a little long. But no matter, for despite this trivial shortcoming, the head was radiant with character. The great forehead, the huge, wide-set, flashing eyes with their pupils the colour of burnt topaz—it is not for nothing that the Arabs call their horses' eyes the Eye of Allah. Indeed everything down to the large, delicately outlined nostrils that he worked ceaselessly imparted to the barb an expression of the utmost pride and fiercest intelligence.

As he continued to work on him with the grooming glove, it was as if Agba was bringing him back to life. As the dirt and dust fell away his coat began to grow darker and darker, with what appeared to be flashes of flame here and there. Agba then started to use another glove made of a sort of heavy velvet with which to bring a shine to the coat. But here all his skill proved in vain. The unfortunate beast had been kept in such miserable, dirty conditions that, rather than become silky with a satin sheen, his coat stayed rough and dull. But for all that, the horse had become unrecognizable. His beautiful long mane that Agba had washed so carefully now appeared to float along his neck, while his tail, like a silken plume, seemed to fall from his ample quarters like a rain of jade.

Doubtless he still bore the signs of his past trials, yet the barb displayed such nobility and quality that even the Quaker, who knew little enough about horses, could not fail to be impressed and said to himself, "When the poor beast has put on some weight, even though he may have scarred knees, he'll make a fine hack for my son-in-law, the minister. The horse seems quiet as a lamb; it's just the way he's been treated that's soured him. Now I can see that God wanted me to make a profit out of my act of charity, and now I'm going to perform another one by saving this poor, wretched mute. A man who can love a horse as he does must have a good heart. It would be too cruel to part them. It simply means there'll be another mouth to feed at Bury Hall."

So the Quaker went ahead with his plan and Agba's joy was boundless as he put the magic amulets around El Scham's neck once more, believing that the influence of the unlucky marking was gone for good and that El Scham would soon accomplish the destiny promised him by the lucky white mark. Thus it was, filled with hope and ambition, that Agba accompanied El Scham and his new master on their homeward journey.

Chapter Five

Bury Hall

BURY HALL, the Quaker's residence, was a delightful country house some fifteen miles west of London on the banks of the Thames. The house was set on a hillside and a glorious, finely tended lawn studded with noble, old trees that swept down to the riverbank. Behind the main house was a fair-size stand of oaks traversed by a winding path that led to the stables and the small home farm that the Quaker looked after himself. The farm buildings, covered in climbing roses, ivy, and honeysuckle were themselves a delight to behold.

This was the calm and charming refuge to which El Scham's lucky star had now led him. Instead of the dark and foul-smelling Parisian lean-to, El Scham now had a large loose-box to himself—whitewashed, with a brick floor that was almost completely covered by a generous layer of straw. It was lit by two shuttered windows (on the north and south sides) which could bring air or warmth, as appropriate, to the stable, in which the shiny wooden manger and the polished, iron hayrack were always abundantly filled. Even the cat, which had travelled with Agba and El Scham, and which the Quaker's servants had christened Grimalkin, was given a little corner to himself, painted green, from which he could observe his friend to his heart's content and keep watch for the local mice on which he waged a war without mercy.

That was not all; the gentle Quaker, out of respect for the close bond between

El Scham and Agba, had built the Arab a little room above the loose-box, from which he could see his beloved charge at any moment of the day or night.

In other words, man, horse and cat had stepped into a different world from the moment they had come to this calm and bountiful dwelling. Grimalkin's thick, shiny fur spoke of good health and repose; he was grown so massive that you could tell at a glance that his merciless mouse war was no more than an amusement, a disinterested and recreational form of hunt.

Agba had abandoned his old burnous, his beard, and his grimy turban. Now he wore leather britches, top boots, a velveteen jacket, and a felt hat. His face had filled out, and even though Arabs never grow fat, he had developed a certain undeniable portliness about his person.

As for El Scham, he was unrecognizable. This is not to say that he had grown

fat any more than Agba, for his conformation was such that he could never get
soft—but rest, loving care, and an excellent diet had restored his coat to all its
glory.

His neck, shoulders, haunches, and
crupper had such a brilliant, black sheen
to them that they glowed, while his
flanks were covered in a fiery red mottle,
and the white mark that had been the
special object of Agba's grateful attentions blended its silvery whiteness with
the rose tones of the foot and pastern,
contrasting with the rest of the leg—
hard, black, and shiny as ebony.

An unappreciative eye would see a single, small flaw, one that might be
thought to mar—nay to negate—all this
perfection, namely the little cluster of
white hair that El Scham sported on
each knee ever since he had scarred
them on the cobblestones of the Rue
Dauphine. Agba had vainly begged his

master to let him use black dye on these marks of disgrace. The Quaker had forbidden him to do so in no uncertain terms, considering the procedure to be a form of mendacious deceit.

This then was the happy and peaceful existence that Agba, El Scham, and Grimalkin had come to enjoy six months after leaving France. But, despite their apparent good fortune, a storm was brewing over the heads of the three friends. For it must be said that despite the Quaker's almost infinite capacity for patience, not to speak of his fondness for Agba, the violent, unrestrained, and wild behavior of El Scham, now fully restored and in the pink of condition, had brought that patience to an end. But reluctant as he was to judge any creature— man or beast—unfairly, it was only after a careful investigation into El Scham's misdeeds that the master of Bury Hall decided to summon Agba to appear before him and other members of the household. It was not that the unfortunate Agba had given the Quaker the slightest reason to be displeased with him, but rather that the Arab was the barb's only advocate.

In early August 1732, the Quaker assembled his daughter, his son-in-law the Reverend Doctor Harrison, and a close friend of the family, Mr. Rogers, proprietor of The Red Lion tavern in Charing Cross. The Quaker had sent his housekeeper Mrs. Cockburn to fetch Agba and the assembled company of judges was awaiting him.

The austere and serious appearance of these players in a domestic drama imparted an air of solemnity to the scene. The Quaker's daughter, a cold and severe twenty-five-year-old beauty, was dressed in a manner of the utmost simplicity and held her child upon her knees. Dr. Harrison, who sat next to her, wore black and had his nose buried deep in his Bible. Mr. Rogers was about forty years old, tall, and slender. The black wig he sported made his stern countenance seem sterner still. His prominent jaw was partly concealed by a high cravat. He wore a long, reddish brown coat with silver buttons, an embroidered cotton waistcoat, deerskin britches, top boots with steel spurs, and was held to be one of the best and boldest riders in the country.

Guessing why she had been sent to fetch Agba, Mrs. Cockburn could scarcely contain her joy. For alas Agba inspired a kind of horror in the servants' hall. The staff did not share their master's tolerance and unbeknownst to that excellent man, they called the unfortunate Agba a Jew, a renegade, a heretic, an untouchable. But the Arab, man of honour as he was, neither could nor would protest. Caring nothing for their spite, and happy to pass the day in the company of El Scham and Grimalkin—notwithstanding their daily bouts of vituperation—he had made his little room into a kind of paradise in which not only could he observe his horse at his leisure after he had groomed him, but he could also dream a thousand dreams of the glorious future that awaited the barb. For Agba, believing more than ever in the lucky omen, held their sojourn in the modest accommodations of the Quaker to be but a staging post on the way to incomparably higher things.

His daydreaming was now interrupted by the harsh voice of Mrs. Cockburn who informed him that his master was waiting to see him in the parlour. Despite his trust in his lucky star, Agba was worried by the sardonic and triumphant smile with which Mrs. Cockburn indicated the parlour door to him. Nevertheless, after a respectful knock, he entered.

As he did so Dr. Harrison shut his Bible, the Quaker and Mr. Rogers interrupted their conversation, and the daughter of the house sat up straighter than ever, adopting an expression of the utmost gravity.

Poor Agba, who had glanced timidly at the assembled company that had always to date treated him with the greatest kindness, was deeply disturbed by their air of magisterial sternness.

He took a particular aversion to Mr. Rogers and twice he lowered his gaze rather than meet the penetrating accusatory stare of the proprietor of The Red Lion, as he looked Agba carefully over, appearing to sneer as he tapped the handle of his whip against his boot.

The Quaker, in his usual calm and gentle voice, asked Agba to step forward.

"My friend, I found you in a condition of wretched poverty and I saved you from it."

Agba gave a deep bow and gestured his appreciation.

"Yes, you have indeed been grateful," replied the Quaker who had come to understand Agba's language of signs. "You have been a good and faithful servant, and it is not you who have given cause for complaint, but the horse."

The Arab expressed his astonishment.

"The horse was in a wretched plight," the Quaker resumed, "But he was one of God's creatures and I took pity on him and took him to my house. I was especially fond of him because on the day I saved him I learnt that my daughter had born me a grandson so that everything associated with that day is especially dear to me. But how has the horse rewarded my generosity?"

Agba gave the Quaker an uncomprehending stare.

"As long as he recalled his recent misfortunes he was gentle and obedient, and

I hoped that my son-in-law would be able to ride him. But you know how he reacted the first time my son-in-law got on his back."

Looking carefully at the Quaker, Agba made a gesture that seemed to represent the sudden soaring flight of a flock of birds, as if to suggest that El Scham had set off at a rapid gallop. That, at least, is how the Quaker understood him, for he continued.

"Yes indeed and he galloped so fast and in such an uncontrollable manner that had it not been for the bog into which my son-in-law had the good fortune to fall, and which slowed the horse down, he could have carried him a further five or six miles, could he not?"

Agba indicated his agreement, but at the same time he raised his hands to the corners of his mouth.

"Yes, yes, I know you had tried to show me that my son-in-law could have controlled the horse with a different bit, but what about the second time? You'd chosen the bit yourself but instead of going forward quietly, the wild thing reared up onto its hind legs and my son-in-law had to dismount by sliding over his quarters or else the beast might have fallen back onto him, might it not?"

Agba indicated his agreement once again, but then, after a moment's pause for thought, and as if overcoming a hesitation, he looked timidly at Dr. Harrison, and gave a violent jerk with his left hand.

"He is suggesting, and I'm sure he's right, that I'm heavy handed and that it was my own fault that the horse reared up," Dr. Harrison observed generously.

"That may be," said the Quaker, "but remember how, before we gave up hope of being able to ride him, we sent him to Tom Stagg the hunt servant, and even though Tom is one of the most skilled horsemen in the county, didn't he keep getting bucked off? And remember the last time, when he couldn't get him off, how he crushed poor Stagg against a wall, making him cry out and forcing him to dismount in a hurry? He did, did he not?"

"Stagg is easily bested," said Mr. Rogers giving a cruel flourish of his whip.

"Send him to me for a couple of days and I'll have the scoundrel supple as a glove."

Agba flashed Mr. Rogers a scornful, sidelong glance, and looked away.

"And is it not true," said the Quaker, "that the horse sent Tom Stagg to bed for a week?"

Agba, whose expression to date had been one of timid submission, suddenly came alive. Pulling his heels together time after time, he flourished his right hand as if he were dealing out blows.

"He means," said the Quaker, "that Stagg kept spurring and beating the

horse, which is true. But gentler methods were getting us nowhere, so we had
to try sterner stuff if we were to tame a
horse that no one seems to be able to
ride."

Agba pointed proudly at himself.

"Yes it is true, you can indeed ride him
all right, and wild as he is, you control
him. But that just goes to prove his contrary nature, because if he listens to you,
if he obeys you like a dog obeys his master,
why is he so impossible with others? When
my son-in-law first tried to ride him, he
didn't beat him; he never showed him the
whip or touched him with a spur. He spoke
to him gently and kindly. He patted him
and stroked him and yet twice the beast
put him on the ground and endangered his
life. Be fair now, can I keep a horse that
only you can ride?"

Agba sunk his head in sadness.

"And that's not all," continued the
Quaker. "The beast is as vicious with

other animals as he is with people. Didn't he nearly tear the ear off my pony, Little Bryony, without being given the least provocation? Didn't he?"

Taking a piece of blank paper from the desk Agba ground his teeth and shook his head to indicate rage.

"I understand. You mean that this devil of yours cannot abide white horses?"

Agba nodded.

"That may be, but what about my other pony, Black, who is dark as a raven's wing, gentle as a dove, and so old and weak he wouldn't harm a fly. Didn't the beast chase him, kick and bite him, that time when you carelessly let him out? What have you to say about that?"

Agba indicated the hat he held in his hand and made the same pantomime of rage.

"So he hates black horses, too. That may be, but that means he hates all horses, for two weeks ago when The Reverend Michael Fitzpatrick hacked over on his bay and you met him on his way home after luncheon on the Richmond Road, pray what happened? Did he not break his halter rope and mount a savage assault upon The Reverend's mare? Is it not true that he reared up, set his forelegs upon poor Fitzpatrick's shoulders, and tore off his hat and wig with his teeth? Finally, for all the control you have over him, did it not require the aid of some passing labourers to extract the minister and his mare from beneath this fiend—and then only with the utmost difficulty. Is this not the case?"

Here the Arab's miming became more elaborate still and was clear enough to bring a blush to the cheeks of the Quaker's decorous daughter, as Agba indicated that it was not wickedness that had set El Scham at the Reverend's mare. Rather he had come under the influence of a far sweeter instinct, one which the Arab tried to specify by making amorous, caressing gestures and smiling with all the gracious delight he could muster.

The Quaker, however, who habitually appeared so calm and benevolent, promptly put an end to Agba's gesticulations with a severe scowl.

The Arab ceased his representations and stood there motionless, awaiting the end of the inquisition with foreboding. He could not help wondering whether the current period of good fortune was over for El Scham despite the amulets he wore round his neck, to be replaced once again by a time of ill omen.

But now, as if reproaching himself for a moment's harshness, the Quaker added in a gentler tone of voice, "I cannot continue to keep the horse at Bury Hall. I sold him for what I paid for him to my friend Rogers here. He is happy to take him on and hopes to tame him and you are to take him to his new quarters in London today. But that does not mean to say that you are dismissed. I am most pleased with you, my friend; you are faithful and intelligent. You may, if you wish, remain in my household. Otherwise I will give you a small sum of money and excellent references in the hope that with God's aid you will find a better master than me."

The Quaker gave a sigh and turned away so as to conceal the tear in his eye, for he was genuinely fond of poor Agba.

Words cannot describe the expression of abject misery with which Agba greeted his sentence. Joining his hands, he knelt at the feet of the Quaker in supplication, then, recognizing that his entreaties were without avail, he turned to Dr. and Mrs. Harrison who were themselves overcome with emotion. But El Scham's misdeeds and his evident uselessness were too much to have the Quaker change his mind.

Turning to Agba with a voice choking with emotion, he said: "My friend, I am always as good as my word. If you wish to remain at Bury Hall you will receive the same treatment you always have. If you choose to leave me, Mrs. Cockburn will give you the sum of money that I spoke of. As for the horse, here is his new master," he said, pointing to Mr. Rogers.

"And this whip will soon teach him that his master is what I really am!" said Mr. Rogers in a cruel tone of voice as he brandished his crop.

"It is the will of Allah, and now comes a time of misfortune," Agba reflected as he left the parlour in a bitter mood.

That very evening Agba and Grimalkin took El Scham to The Red Lion, forever leaving the calm and peaceful life of Bury Hall. Although Mr. Rogers had brutally dismissed his offer to act as El Scham's groom, Agba was determined not to abandon his charge, especially now that he was in the hands of such a cruel owner.

Chapter Six

At the Sign of The Red Lion

IT WAS OVER A MONTH since Agba and Grimalkin had left Bury Hall. For the first time in seven years, that is to say since he was foaled, he had gone thirty-two days—he counted them one by one—without seeing the barb.

He had carried out the Quaker's instructions and taken Agba to London. At the gateway to The Red Lion he had handed him over to a grey-haired, old groom wearing leather britches and a scarlet coat, who seized El Scham's halter rope and made it clear to Agba in no uncertain terms that he was needed no longer.

Chapter Six

Thus Agba remained in London, without a position and virtually penniless. However his extraordinary attachment to the barb made him indifferent to his plight. He planned to eke out the Quaker's modest sum and then survive by begging. Wanting above all else to stay as close to El Scham as possible, Agba had purchased the right to spend his nights in a corner of a stable close by The Red Lion, a corner that he shared with his loyal friend, Grimalkin, who survived hunting the mice that, alas, were no longer the objects of mere sport but had become his only form of sustenance.

Located in the Charing Cross Road, the tavern had extensive outbuildings and its stables were to be found in a small side street. Agba had supposed that by staying nearby and lending a helping hand to Mr. Rogers's stable lads, he might be able to see El Scham occasionally and guide him through this period of ill fortune while waiting for better things to come. But alas it soon proved that Agba was sadly mistaken.

The day after he had handed El Scham over, Agba, hoping he might bribe one of the lads with a glass or too, took a little money with him and went to the stable door of The Red Lion. There he was met by the same old groom who had taken El Scham from him, who asked him angrily what it was that he wanted. It was in vain that the mute tried to use sign language to indicate that he wanted to see the horse, in vain that he showed him a florin and went through the motions of downing a glass of ale. Feigning incomprehension, the old man gave him short shrift.

"You see this house, do you, you gallows bird? If you ever come here again, we'll soon teach you to be sorry you ever did, just see if we won't."

He slammed the door without further ado and went off cursing.

A disappointed and sorrowful Agba, puzzled by the groom's bad temper but unwilling to abandon all hope of seeing El Scham, lingered in the street outside the stable. He was wondering what to do next when the door opened again to let out two men carrying a litter.

Drawing closer, Agba could see that it contained a man who seemed badly hurt and he heard one of the bearers say, "God damn the horse what did this to poor Johnny."

"I warned Mr. Rogers, didn't I," replied Johnny in a voice so faint it could scarcely be heard.

"So what did you tell him then, Johnny, my son?" answered the litter bearer.

"The moment I laid eyes on that broken-kneed bastard what isn't worth ten guineas, I told Mr. Rogers that he had a wicked look about him. And then this morning, before I could even lay a brush on him, he goes and fetches me two in the ribs."

"My dear, gentle El Scham," thought the Arab. "That's my horse. I always knew you'd never let anyone groom you but me."

"Don't you worry, Johnny," the second litter bearer said. "Mr. Rogers swore by his whip and spurs that the quad is going to pay. And I wouldn't want to be wearing his shoes. Mr. Rogers is a hard man at best and I never seen him so angry with a horse."

The litter moved on and Agba could hear no more.

The next morning at daybreak Agba was on the lookout again, hanging around by the stable door. To his astonishment this opened yet again to let out yet another litter. The Arab drew near, and even though the bearers were silent, it was obvious that it contained another of El Scham's victims in sore need of medical attention.

Although he was proud of his horse and his refusal to let strangers groom him, Agba shuddered at the thought of Mr. Rogers's reaction and his anxiety grew by the hour.

Nothing more transpired that day or the next. No more litters emerged and the stable door remained closed all day. Agba had hoped at the very least to see someone lead the horse out, but all to no avail. In the meantime, all his plans to make his way into the stable or even catch a glimpse of his horse through an open door came to nothing. The miserable, old groom was always there to keep him away.

Over a month passed like this, with Agba experiencing indescribable worry and alarm. In his ignorance of El Scham's fate, he sometimes thought that Mr. Rogers might have killed him in a fit of rage, but then he would at least have seen his body being carted out. At other times, giving in to an even darker despair, he supposed that El Scham had grown used to being groomed by strangers and had forgotten him. The very possibility reduced him to positive paroxysms of jealous rage. But then he took comfort in the thought that if the horse had been tamed he would have been ridden out, and he had not made an appearance for over a month.

As he grew more and more puzzled he said to himself that perhaps El Scham had fallen ill, and his misery and worry redoubled at the thought. El Scham ill and tended by strangers, bereft of his lucky amulets! The idea was intolerable.

What more was there to say? Things could not go on as they were. After thirty-two days spent in doubt and ignorance, Agba, no longer able to resist the compelling urge to see what had happened to El Scham, decided to try to break into the yard.

He picked a dark and rainy night in early autumn when the adjoining street was empty. At ten o'clock he drew near to the stable door and listened, but heard nothing but a kind of muted and distant throbbing sound. Feeling that the time was not yet ripe he decided to wait.

In order to scale the eight-foot stable wall he had created a primitive rope ladder consisting of a knotted rope with an iron rod at one end that he had bent into a hook. He planned to throw this improvised grappling iron over the wall and shin up the rope.

Unaware that his plan could get him into grave trouble with the law, he awaited an opportune moment to carry it out. As the clocks struck eleven, he could hear the night watchman call out and concealed himself as he passed. Unable to restrain his impatience any longer he managed to set his grappling iron on the third attempt, climbed quickly to the top of the wall, and tried to gain his bearings. But the night was so dark that he could make out nothing. Deciding to take his chances, he slid down the rope on the far side of the wall.

His heart was beating fast as he reached the ground, and he could now hear what had once been a distant throb more distinctly and groped his way toward it. Hugging the wall he reached the entrance to a kind of passage at the end of which he could see light coming from some cracks in a door. Pausing for an instant, he now realized that the sound he had previously heard was the beat of a drum. Holding his breath he made his way along the corridor and looked through a crack in the door.

It was with a mixture of joy, horror, and an unmitigated loathing of Mr. Rogers that he recognized his beloved El Scham in a state that nearly broke his heart!

Chained to a hay rack in such a way
that he was obliged to keep his head up,
he had fetters on his legs and his movement was further restricted by a rope
round his quarters fastened to two iron
rings. He was thin enough to bring tears
to Agba's eyes and his sides bore numerous welts. He seemed almost too weak to
stand and appeared to have been ill,
since the number of pins with horsehair
knots round their heads that were stuck
in his neck and the large vein of the
stomach (which the English used to use
to bleed their horses) suggested that he
had been liberally bled.

On the wall hung a number of objects
that appeared to Agba to be instruments
of torture: bridles and bits of barbaric
severity, a tack noseband, a twitch. But
worse than any of these to his eyes were
the actions of the old groom, who obsti-
nately beat upon his drum every time
that the wretched El Scham, who was ex-

hausted and overcome with fatigue, attempted to sleep.

It seemed to Agba that the time that El Scham had spent between the shafts had been a kind of paradise compared to the hell to which his unlucky star had now brought him. Seeing him in such a pitiable condition, he was as if paralysed. Two great tears rolled down his cheek and he remained standing there staring fixedly at his love.

Suddenly he was aroused from his lethargy by the sound of several sets of approaching footsteps. With no other way out of the passage he was caught like a rat in a trap. As the footsteps drew closer, accompanied by the glimmer of a lantern, he looked desperately for a way out—the light growing stronger as he heard Mr. Rogers's mocking, sadistic voice.

"We'll soon see if my latest arrangement has finally tamed the obstinate quad."

Chapter Six

Agba made a last bid for freedom. Moving with lightning speed he threw himself at Mr. Rogers, hoping to dash the lantern from his hand and escape into the darkness. In fact, just as the proprietor of The Red Lion, seeing something move in the darkness, was saying, "What the devil," Agba sprang at him like a panther, knocked him against the wall, and ran on down the passage. Alas Mr. Rogers was accompanied by a servant who ran after Agba with a cry of "Stop thief!" He was joined in the hue and cry by another servant, by the old groom, and also by Mr. Rogers who was back on his feet. Running for his life, Agba made his way back to his rope and was half way up the wall when someone seized his leg in a grip of iron and dragged him to the ground.

The old groom and the other servants gave Agba a severe beating and then Mr. Rogers, holding a lantern to his face, discovered the identity of the midnight intruder.

"So it's you, is it, you wretched tramp. You've been hanging about the place for weeks planning to rob me haven't you? Well, well, well, it's a stout cord and the gallows for you, my lad, and they won't be long acoming."

Then, turning to his servants, "You tie him up careful now for he's slippery as an eel, and take him to the magistrate."

Bound hand and foot, the unfortunate Agba was immediately brought before the authorities, accompanied by Mr. Rogers who took with him the rope and grappling iron as evidence of an attempt at breaking and entering, a most serious charge for which Agba would have to answer to the officers of the law.

Chapter Seven

Prison

BEFORE RELATING what happened to Agba when he appeared before the magistrate, an explanation is required for the extraordinary treatment to which Mr. Rogers had subjected El Scham.

As an innkeeper, Mr. Rogers always had a large number of post chaises and carriages for hire in his yard. He knew his horseflesh and was an excellent rider. Much taken by the Quaker's tales of El Scham's untameable nature, sheer vanity had prompted him to try to master him. The first thing he did was to keep the

Arab away from the barb to break the bond between them, while treating the animal as kindly and gently as possible. But the fates that befell Johnny and his companion made it abundantly clear that a change of approach was called for.

Mr. Rogers then tried to break El Scham and tame his indomitable character by starving the barb, who, since the departure of Agba and Grimalkin, appeared to become wilder and more vicious by the day. In order to avoid his being able to kick or bite, he was fettered, his feed was cut steadily back, and he was often bled. At first this seemed to work. As he grew weaker he began to allow other stablehands to groom him and even let Mr. Rogers get on his back and school him in his yard, which had been covered in a thick layer of straw.

But the moment Mr. Rogers, encouraged by these signs of progress, ordered his feed to be increased, El Scham was soon back to his old tricks. And one day, after he had tried and failed to buck Mr. Rogers off, he reared, threw his rider against a wall, and nearly succeeded in crushing him.

Mr. Rogers was a stubborn man who refused to admit defeat. Determined to master the horse, he cut back on his feed again and arranged for the ministrations of his groom to keep him deprived of sleep. This was the situation in which Agba found him shortly before being caught red-handed and taken before a magistrate.

The evidence against him was so overwhelming that Agba could entertain no hope of avoiding his fate. Besides, being jealous of Agba's unique ability to control the otherwise untameable horse, and driven by a spiteful sense of envy that was miserable enough (if all too human), Mr. Rogers said nothing that might mitigate the severity of the charges, making no mention of the unfortunate Arab's extraordinary love for his horse.

Charged with breaking and entering with an intent to rob, Agba was taken from the magistrate's house to Newgate Prison where he was to be held until his trial.

As chance would have it, the Quaker's housekeeper Mrs. Cockburn was a cousin of one of the gaolers, from whom she learned of Agba's plight. Bad-tempered though she might be, Mrs. Cockburn was not actually malevolent. When she heard that Agba was accused of breaking, entering, and attempted burglary, she promptly declared that the charges could not possibly be true. Yes, the Arab was a heathen, destined to roast in hell forever, but it must nevertheless be admitted that the heathen in question was totally incapable of doing anything dishonest and that he had undoubtedly scaled the wall in an attempt to see his horse, which the wretched man and the cat Grimalkin both loved to distraction. To lend further credence to her contention, Mrs. Cockburn told her cousin a whole series of tales about the peculiar attachment of Agba to the horse and of the horse to Agba, adding that she had no doubt that Old Nick, in other words the devil himself, had had his part to play in the matter.

The gaoler was sufficiently moved by these stories and by Agba's plight to urge his cousin to tell the Quaker what had happened. But fearing that her master would take him back into his service after rescuing him, she elected to keep silent and Bury Hall continued to know nothing about the Arab's misfortune. However, thanks to his cousin's revelations, the gaoler began to take an interest in his prisoner.

In the meantime, in response to Mr. Rogers's complaint, the magistrate began his investigation. He questioned the

groom who had let Agba stay in a corner
of a loose box and a search was made of
his belongings—a search that did not
take long. All they found was his old
burnous, El Scham's two grooming
gloves, a comb, and a kind of ointment
used to detangle the mane and tail. As
for El Scham's pedigree and his magic
amulets, Agba had kept them on his person, bitterly regretting that he had been
unable to place them around the horse's
neck in the hope that they might bring
about a change of luck.

In the course of their search, the magistrate's men had come across Grimalkin, lying on the old camel hair sack
in which his master kept his treasures—
treasures that the cat was ready to defend. But it was in vain that he dug his
claws into the bag and slashed one of the
magistrate's men across the hand. He
too was arrested and taken to Newgate
Prison in the sack that he had tried to

keep out of the reach of the long arm of the law.

An unhappy man can take comfort in the smallest consolation. Agba was overcome with joy when, as he was being asked to identify his possessions, the gaoler came into his cell bringing the faithful Grimalkin with him in his arms.

But although he was happy to be reunited with his companion, Agba began to succumb to the most all-embracing and overpowering depression. It was in vain that the gaoler would sometimes bring him little food parcels sent up by Mrs. Cockburn, who felt sorry for Agba in her fashion, even though she continued to say nothing about his plight. Grimalkin was the only one to partake of these delicacies; Agba scarcely ate anything and was visibly wasting away.

His cell was small and dark, lit by a small barred window set high in the wall. The Arab spent his days sitting on the hard, wooden bed, his head on his knees, or staring up at the window with his dark and tearful eyes trying to glimpse an occasional patch of blue, stroking Grimalkin with one hand, and clasping El Scham's amulets to his chest in silent rage with the other.

He had never been in a graver situation: alone in the world; far from home; charged with a serious crime and unable to defend himself; with no one to understand why he had done what he did, since no Englishman could appreciate the depth of his feelings for the horse. Supposing himself into the bargain forever parted from El Scham, Agba's melancholy, now turned into hopeless and unmitigated despair.

Stoic and resigned, he accepted his fate without protest, a fate shared by El Scham, who, he believed, could never survive the cruel treatment meted out by Mr. Rogers. Although he had the

Muslim horror of suicide, he decided to put an end to his miserable existence in the hope that he might soon find himself in the great pastures of paradise reunited with his beloved El Scham as proud and fair as ever. In other words he decided to hang himself with the silken cord that bore the details of El Scham's pedigree.

But first he gave a last thought to his horse, to his country, and to El Scham's days of glory. He recalled him as he might recall an apparition—with steel and gold shining beneath his purple housing. He saw him in an oasis, neighing with flaring nostrils as he breathed the perfumed air of evening, pawing the desert sand impatiently, or resting in the shadow of his master's tent. For the last time he saw him as a sultan, reigning over a harem of submissive white mares, anxious to bear the glorious foals that destiny had appeared to promise the mighty El Scham by marking him with the lucky white mark.

Tortured beyond endurance by these memories of past happiness, Agba climbed onto his bed, attached the silken cord to one of the bars on the window and slipped his head into the noose he had formed with the other end.

At that very moment the cell door swung suddenly open.

Chapter Eight

The Visit

$\mathbb{S}$TARTLED BY the unexpected noise, Agba could not go through with his plan. But his surprise, his embarrassment, his wretched demeanour, and the silk cord hanging from the window, all spoke all too clearly of his desperate intent.

It was almost dark and the newcomers, brilliantly lit by the gaoler's torch, presented a strange and luminous contrast to the prison darkness. In the vanguard was a woman of considerable stature, about seventy years old, with a majestic expression that belied her age. Simply clad in a dress of brown satin, she carried a King

Charles Spaniel under her left arm. Her right arm leaned upon that of a much younger man who was magnificently dressed in the French fashion, in a blue velvet coat trimmed in gold with cuffs of lace that were so long and so magnificent that they almost entirely concealed his be-jewelled fingers. White silk embroideries, a plumed hat, and red heeled shoes completed the attire of a gentleman whose elegance would have been a match for the finest lord at the court of France.

The noble lady was Sarah Jennings, Duchess of Marlborough, widow of the famous John Churchill, the first Duke, who had remained so faithful to his memory that she had once answered the Earl of Somerset, who had proposed marriage to her, thus: "Even if I were thirty years old and not sixty, I would not permit the emperor of the world to occupy the place that the Duke of Marlborough will always hold in my heart."

Charitable and pious, having turned her back on all her past glories in favour of good works, Her Grace often visited prisons, concerning herself with the crimes and misdeeds of their inmates, and taking a special interest in those who had decided to repent and mend their ways or whose wretched plight otherwise inspired her pity.

The young man at the duchess's side was her son-in-law, Francis Leonard, the second Earl of Godolphin, son of the famous Sidney, Viscount Realton and Earl Godolphin, Lord Treasurer of England, who had played such an important part in the revolution of 1688 and had died in 1710. That day he was accompanying his mother-in-law on one of her regular visits to Newgate Prison.

The silk cord still dangling from the window frame and Agba's haggard expression made his intentions all too apparent, while his foreign appearance and his inability to speak all helped move the duchess to pity. She asked the prison director her usual question.

"Pray what crime has this man committed?"

Fortunately for Agba, Mrs. Cockburn's cousin was a gossip. The story of a groom scaling a stable wall just to see his horse had become one of the touching tales of Newgate Prison and the director told it in a way that portrayed Agba in the most favorable light possible. The duchess was moved to tears and her son-in-law Godolphin was overcome with admiration for Agba and for the horse.

Noting the visitors' sympathetic interest, the gaoler ventured to whisper to the prison director that he was sure the Quaker of Bury Hall would vouch for the Arab and attest that he was totally incapable of theft or any kind of dishonest action and that, if needs be, the entire Quaker household would confirm the assertion.

The director relayed this information to the duchess who, delighted at finding a deserving cause, asked him to give her some written information about Agba. In the meantime, Lord Godolphin swore that once the Arab was free from prison and his horse free of The Red Lion, the two of them would never again leave Gogmagog, his Cambridgeshire stud.

Trembling, disturbed, and unresponsive to all that was taking place—since he could not believe it had anything to do with him—Agba, who suddenly felt extremely weak, stood (or rather leant) against the cell wall with downcast eyes.

"Does the poor wretch understand English?" asked the duchess.

"Aye, Your Grace, he understands well enough."

She turned to Agba and addressed him in the kindest, gentlest tone of voice.

"My friend, you nearly committed a terrible crime by seeking to put an end to your life. You lost your faith in Providence, and yet Providence has come to your aid. Your tale has aroused my interest and you can count upon my support and upon the fairness of your judges. Here, this is for you. Take heart and put your trust in God."

As she spoke she gave the Arab two golden guineas that he contemplated with a kind of dull amazement.

"And my friend, I can promise that once you are out of the clutches of the law, you and the horse you love so much will have homes for life at Gogmagog. By Heavens what you've done will be an example to everyone there and show them what loving a horse really means. So here are two guineas more to buy your horse a new bridle. I am going to send for Rogers and pay him whatever he wants for the barb so that the two of you will never be parted again!"

The duchess beckoned and Lord Godolphin escorted her from the cell. The torches left with the departing visitors and the cell door slammed shut, leaving Agba alone with Grimalkin wondering whether it had all been a dream. Yet the clink of the gold coins in his pocket convinced him it had really happened. He began to take in some of what had been said to him. "Never parted again," "Pay him whatever he wants." The words had such an extraordinary ring to them that poor Agba still did not dare believe that they had actually been spoken.

If all this really happened, he thought, perhaps their luck had changed at last.

What more was there to be said? The Duchess of Marlborough and the Earl of Godolphin were as good as their word.

When Agba appeared in court, the Quaker appeared as witness for the defense. He and his son-in-law had come to town as soon as they learned of Agba's plight. His acquittal was made easier by the express demand of Mr. Rogers himself, who was delighted to be rid of a beast as fractious as El Scham, which he sold to Lord Godolphin for twenty-five guineas.

The moment Agba was free, he went to thank his benefactor, who granted him the privilege of going to The Red Lion to fetch El Scham himself. The stablemen were delighted to see the creature go as they had not forgotten the damage he'd done to Johnny and his colleague. A triumphant Agba, eyes filled with tears, was quick to release his horse from the vile fetters and ties that had restricted his movement.

When he sensed he was free, El Scham looked hard at Agba, then he shook his head, set his ears back, and approached his old friend. At first he was somewhat wary, then he halted for a moment and gave a kind of fearful whinny. As he did so, he flared his huge nostrils and this, together with the concern and astonishment reflected in his enormous eyes, imparted an expression of quite extraordinary intelligence to his noble head.

Agba thereupon clapped his hands in a special way and the horse bounded toward him. There could no longer be any doubt; it really was his friend. He reared a little and then, arching his supple neck, he came up to Agba and rubbed his head against him, asking for a scratch.

Once he was past his initial delight, Agba's first task was to place the lucky charms and pedigree around El Scham's neck once more and to plant a pious kiss on the lucky white mark. He then put a saddle and bridle on his charge and the two of them set off, shaking the dust of The Red Lion from their feet. Weak though he was, El Scham seemed happy to bear the weight of his rider, pawed the ground, and gave joyous little bucks as the two of them made their way to meet Lord Godolphin who was awaiting them in his stable yard.

Even without the prejudice that the English then held against barbs and Arabs, it must be said that El Scham's lamentable condition and the signs of ill treatment that he bore did little enough to commend him. At the moment of his triumphant arrival in the yard, Lord Godolphin was talking with a youngish man, built like a jockey, wearing a green coat trimmed with gold, deerskin britches, and travelling boots. He had a thinnish face with an ironic expression somewhat marred by the fact that he had lost his teeth.

"Pull him up," Lord Godolphin said to Agba, who halted El Scham and sat tall in the saddle, proud as an emperor.

"Take a look at this one, Chifney!" Lord Godolphin said to the little man, who was none other than the head groom of the Gogmagog Stud.[1]

"So, what do you think?"

"I believe your lordship said that this fellow is the only one who can ride him or drive him?"

"Yes, yes, but what do you think of him?"

"Pretty good legs, decent conformation, and a truly ugly head; He's a real barb all right. What does his lordship want done with the animal?"

"Bless my soul, I don't know. I just felt sorry for the poor wretch and his horse. I didn't think about what to do with it. But anyway, since the horse is good for nothing we'll just turn it out at Gogmagog

---

1. Sam Chifney founded a racing dynasty. His son Sam was the leading jockey of his age and was stable jockey to the Prince of Wales, the future King George IV. Sam's elder son William was an outstanding trainer, while the younger, also named Sam, was the leading jockey of his time. A great nephew, Frank Butler, won the Epsom Derby on West Australian in 1853.

and you'll find the fellow something to do
in the stable. The way he loves horses,
he's bound to be useful."

"Might his lordship permit me to
make a suggestion?"

"By all means."

"His lordship may recall that we need
a new teaser for Hobgoblin? With his
lordship's permission, I think the barb
would suit admirably."

"Good gracious, Chifney, what a capi-
tal idea. Quite right, of course he'll suit."
Then, turning to Agba, "You're to go
with Chifney here and do everything he
tells you."

Agba responded with the deepest of
bows, and set off after the head groom.
Yet if he had had an inkling of the hate-
ful job that El Scham would be called
upon to perform he would a thousand
times rather have seen him back with
Mr. Rogers, or even die a painful and lin-
gering death.

Chapter Nine

Gogmagog

KNOWING NOTHING OF Lord Godolphin's plans for El Scham's future, the next morning Agba set off for Gogmagog mounted on a bay pony—the only colour El Scham would tolerate. The stallion walked at his side, with the cat Grimalkin lounging contentedly on his back—much to the amusement of the passersby.

The party was led by Chifney, and Agba, who saw in him the representative of Lord Godolphin, did his utmost to be of service both to him and to the horses. His conduct was all the more praiseworthy because Chifney took every opportunity to poke sarcastic fun at El Scham. But the Arab responded to these sallies not at all, treating them with a proud disdain.

Now that he had seen El Scham twice saved from a disastrous fate, while he himself had been rescued from death's door by the seemingly miraculous intervention of a duchess, Agba's faith in El Scham's ultimate good fortune had grown unshakable. He had decided henceforth to submit blindly and fearlessly to whatever the future might hold, convinced that no matter what ordeals might lie ahead, El Scham was bound for glory.

However it must be said that this blind faith in the horse's lucky star had been established en route for Gogmagog, long before Agba discovered the odious role for which El Scham was now destined. In the meantime he was at a loss to know what use his charge might possibly be put to. Certainly the stallion had given such convincing proof that only one man could ride him that it was most unlikely that there were any plans to use him under saddle or have anyone but Agba care for him. Yet Agba occasionally allowed himself to entertain the faintest glimmer of an idea that offered such an extraordinary guarantee of El Scham's future greatness that he scarcely dared give it credence, particularly in view of the low esteem in which El Scham appeared to be held. And yet there was the white mark that seemed to promise the most glorious destiny for him and for his progeny. In a word, Agba's wildest hope was that Lord Godolphin would have El Scham stand at his stud.

Nevertheless he had to admit that although the barb was being well treated, he was not enjoying the kind of meticulous attentions that are directed toward a prize stallion. Moreover he kept hearing

Chifney lavish extravagant praise upon a certain Hobgoblin, the only stallion standing at Gogmagog.

As Chifney would have it, there wasn't a sire to be found who could equal Hobgoblin, for he regularly imparted his outstanding strength, speed, and beauty to crop after crop of colts and fillies. Moreover he was helping to restore the quality of English bloodstock, which, as some said, was beginning to lose a purity once achieved by crossing English bloodstock with horses that the crusaders had brought back from the Middle East.

Yet Hobgoblin was no barb. Although he was good looking enough and had won a number of races at Newmarket, there was not a hint of Arab about his conformation. But in those days such was the prejudice against barbs and Arabs that, rather than go back to those original bloodlines in their attempt to improve a degenerating breed, English breeders preferred to have recourse to distant descendants of the Arab, the products of generations of often inappropriate crossbreeding. Hobgoblin, the stallion Lord Godolphin believed was going to be the saviour of English bloodstock, was a case in point. Accordingly his owner sent him the best mares he could find and every member of his harem had to combine the finest conformation with superb breeding. His lordship had just paid six hundred guineas for an exceptional future broodmare named Roxana, whose reputation for speed, strength, and beauty was without equal. By Bald Galloway, she was out of an Ancaster Turk [1] mare.

Always nervy, high strung, and mareish, Roxana was still recovering from the effects of her final race at Newmarket and had not yet arrived at Gogmagog.

---

1. Also known as Lord Carlisle's White Turk.

Nevertheless Chifney could not stop rhapsodizing about her extraordinary quality and the high hopes Lord Godolphin entertained of their future progeny.

Everything that Chifney had recounted on the journey had served to bring Agba to a single conclusion, namely that he thoroughly detested Hobgoblin and, all prejudice aside, deemed El Scham a thousand times his superior thanks to the exceptional quality and nobility of his bloodlines. In his opinion—and he was right—any quality displayed by Hobgoblin was to be explained by his having a minuscule drop of that rich pure Arab blood that coursed unadulterated through the veins of El Scham.

When they reached Gogmagog, Chifney told Agba to put his stallion in a large, airy loose-box even finer than the one at Bury Hall, while Agba had a room close by. So far everything seemed to suggest that their lucky star remained in command.

Lord Godolphin's stud, meticulously and lavishly maintained as it was, did not hold Agba's attention for long, so eager was he to cast a jealous eye over Hobgoblin, the resident sultan of the establishment.

He was admitted to the presence the following day as Chifney himself deigned to conduct him to the celebrated stallion's loose-box, or rather to his palace. For whereas stallions in certain English stud farms still stand in extravagantly luxurious surroundings, in those days the luxury was sometimes taken to that level at which the sublime merged with the ridiculous.

As he conducted him toward Hobgoblin's box, Chifney turned to Agba with an expression combining scorn and disdain, observing smugly that he was about to see what a real stallion looked like. Agba swallowed the insult and followed the head groom without protest.

Hobgoblin resided in a huge separate building in the middle of a yard covered with a thick bed of fine, meticulously raked sand, the scene of his daily exercise. The entrance to the actual stable was a kind of hall, its facade dressed with a blue marble portico supported by two hippogriffs in the midst of which "HOB-GOBLIN!!!" was spelt out in golden lettering with the exclamation marks adding a note of impertinent triumph.

The entire stable was paved in the finest light pink brick, which was so meticulously oiled that it took on the sheen of delicate porcelain. The only decoration on the white plaster walls was a series of bas-reliefs in the classical manner, reproductions of the Cavalcade of the Parthenon.

After the hallway came a huge room with carved oak panelling inlaid with holly, which shone like silver against its dark background. The inlaywork was remarkably fine and delicate, consisting of arabesques based on the designs of Keller, the famous French cabinetmaker, framing beautifully executed depictions of centaurs and horses' heads. Above the paneling, the walls were covered in cloth of Lincoln green, decorated with the Godolphin coat of arms, and hung with a series of paintings by Morier depicting Hobgoblin in all his moments of triumph: in the pasture, in the stable, before and after his races. On either side of the door a couple of glass-fronted shrines lined with crimson velvet displayed the silver and gold cups Hobgoblin had won, together with the racing plates, saddle, bit, and bridle that his jockey used in his races. Two grooms in livery were always on duty in the room, attentive to Hobgoblin's every movement, observing him through two large windows, covered with a fine bronze mesh on the loose-box side.

Dazzled by these wonders, yet convinced that El Scham was a thousand times more entitled to inhabit such a palace, Agba followed Chifney who took a malicious delight in observing the Arab's astonishment.

At last the heavy curtains lavishly embroidered with the Godolphin coat of arms were pushed aside on their rods and the carved double doors leading into the loose box slid aside into their pockets— the doors were designed like that for fear that the stallion might hurt himself against doors that swung open and shut—and Agba could behold the reigning monarch in all his glory.

Hobgoblin had been lolling on a thick bed of soft straw. He gave a scornful glance at the intruders and clambered slowly to his feet. Hobgoblin was a grey with a black mane. Like all stallions standing at stud he had a lot of extra weight on him, the result of generous feeding, and this made it even harder than is the case with any grey to make out his conformation. True, his legs seemed disproportionately slight, however he had a lovely, small, broad head, which was full of expression and character.

The lower half of the loose box was upholstered in cushions of Cordovan leather, stuffed with horsehair and fixed to the walls with small gilded nails. The rest of the walls were covered in a green cloth that matched the brownish tones of the leather perfectly and provided the perfect background to set off Hobgoblin's shining light coat.

Two corners of the box held bronze hayracks, the other two contained mangers fit for a Roman emperor, covered with a thick layer of silver plate. Through two outside windows, also covered in fine, bronze mesh, could be seen Hobgoblin's summer pasture: a magnificent parklike meadow, covered with clover, watered by a clear flowing stream and dotted with clumps of mature trees.

Much as he admired such magnificence, Agba could not help comparing it with the modest circumstances in which El Scham found himself, feeling more than ever that Hobgoblin was a pretender who had no right to enjoy such palatial accommodations.

He still did not know how the stud proposed to use his horse and, apart from his scornful dislike of Hobgoblin, Agba had never been happier. He groomed and rode El Scham as he wanted so that the barb was beginning to recover from his privations while both he and Grimalkin were starting to put on a little weight and their coats were beginning to shine again.

All was well for the moment; it was not until the arrival of Roxana, some months later, that disaster struck again.

Chapter Ten

Roxana

SPRING CAME EARLY in 1733 and the weather was magnificent. Lord Godolphin and some friends who were staying with him at Gogmagog could not wait for Roxana to arrive. Flighty and extremely impressionable, the mare had nothing vicious about her, but she was so highly strung and jumpy that she required the most careful treatment. Loud noises or sudden movements made her start and tremble. But she was also full of spirit and fiercely competitive. When she raced she was so aggressive toward the rest of the field and their jockeys, that she had to be blindfolded and be the last horse to be brought to the starting line. (There was another compelling reason for that blindfold that we will come to in due course.) But the moment the starter dropped his flag she focused all her anger and energy on a determination to win, aided by her strength, her great heart, an amazing turn of foot, and the resolve not to be beat.

Her remarkable character and intelligence were reflected in the circumstances of her training. In those days, horses in training usually used to be ridden out covered in rugs of varying weight known as "sweats" that were sometimes removed to simulate the conditions of an actual race. The trainer would gradually increase the weight of the rugs under which they were galloped to make them sweat off the last ounces of surplus weight.

In her first season Roxana put up with these training methods and all the other racing preliminaries and won her race easily at Newmarket. But she was so intelligent and highly strung that when she went into training the following season, she immediately understood that she was going to race again and became so overwrought, whether out of impatience or a fear that she might lose her race, that she stopped eating or sleeping and lost condition fast. When they galloped her, her connections were dismayed to discover that she was the shadow of her former self.

But with that intelligent understanding derived from years of experience and close observation that marks a true horse lover, Roxana's owner finally determined why she was doing so badly. He changed her regime in such a way that she could never tell when she was about to race. He stopped galloping her in rugs, stopped cutting back on her water as they did on race days, stopped regular shoeing with racing plates, and did not allow the lads to braid her mane. Soon he was delighted to see that she stopped fretting and started to eat up and get her condition back. Then one day, when he thought she was ready, he took her out to the gallops.

The filly did not have time to wear herself out worrying. Instead she concentrated completely on the business at hand and finished ahead of the rest of the string. Nevertheless, she experienced something like the stress she used to feel in an actual race and took a few days to recover from the trial.

Her owner now recognized just how highly strung she really was, but still had the highest opinion of her abilities. Accordingly he continued to try to trick her and give her no inkling of his plans. He took her to Newmarket on race day and led her onto the course in a blindfold that he only removed moments before the start.

As had been the case in her trial, she won her race with ease, but took even longer to get over it. Lord Godolphin bought her as a broodmare when she was in the process of recovering from winning her third and final start. Now she was about to arrive at Gogmagog to be covered by the thrice-lucky Hobgoblin—thrice lucky because such was the extraordinary beauty of the incomparable Roxana that she would have been a worthy match for the stallion of the prophet Mahomet himself.

When she arrived at Gogmagog escorted by Chifney, she was covered in a luxurious, green, traveling rug. All that could be seen through the openings in her hood were two huge, black eyes—radiant, a little wary, yet ablaze with fire and intelligence—two dark pink tinted nostrils that were constantly in movement, and full red lips. The gentle movement of her broad haunches and her fine, free-striding

legs set her emblazoned traveling rug
a-swaying, like a Spanish girl makes her
skirts sway as she walks.

As they tried to make out her appearance beneath her traveling rug, Lord
Godolphin's friends, who had never seen
her before, must have felt as one does at
a costume ball at the sight of a pair of radiant dark eyes staring out enigmatically
from behind a mask.

Lord Godolphin was not quite sure
whether to let his friends witness the un-
robing of Roxana (so that they would
come to appreciate her step-by-step) or
whether he should keep them back until
she was completely unveiled and stood
there like Venus Aphrodite. He finally
decided on the latter course, whispered a
word or two to Chifney, and led his
guests back to the house from where the
dinner bell was calling them.

Poor Agba had been admiring the little there was to be seen of Roxana more

than anyone. For the first time since he had left North Africa, he had experienced that unmistakable surge of emotion that every horseman knows when they find themselves in the presence of true equine beauty and greatness. It was like a stroke of fate, and Agba, who had identified so totally with his own horse, was almost frightened to discover that he was beginning to admire Roxana and want her for El Scham with an urgency that bordered on naked passion. Not for a moment did he think the barb unworthy of her. On the contrary, he could not conceive of a more perfect union. It was rather that he had the terrible foreboding that it would be the common upstart Hobgoblin and not his El Scham who would get to cover this treasure.

Feeling melancholy and not a little jealous, Agba went and joined El Scham and Grimalkin, wisely preferring not to assist at the unveiling of the incomparable

Roxana, a spectacle that might have driven him closer still to despair at the thought that his El Scham might be considered not good enough for her.

Lord Godolphin tantalized his guests by delaying Roxana's debut until the following day. It was ten o'clock in the morning and the sun was shining bright upon the great paddock to which he had ordered Roxana brought, knowing full well that a horse looks its best in bright sunlight on a field of green. It was there that she finally made her entrance, led by Chifney in person.

After a long and appreciative silence, what began as a faint murmur of appreciation grew to a veritable crescendo of praise. No longer wearing any kind of rug, Roxana made her appearance in a light bridle of golden silk—its only ornament, two tufts of the same colour on the browband.

Bathed in sunlight as she was, it is almost impossible to describe the mare's colour. It varied from milky white with tints of silver or vermilion, depending on whether she was in light or shade. Her flanks were tinged with a pinkish hue, her great eyes and her nostrils had a blue grey border, while her flowing tail, mane, and pasterns were a darker shade of grey touched with red that set off the stunning whiteness of her neck.

As she grew accustomed to the spacious paddock and felt the spring breezes blowing through her mane, her veins began to swell with blood and throb blue beneath her satin skin. Flexing her delicate neck like a swan, she started to walk—or rather float—across the green turf, so that the grass seemed scarcely to bend beneath her delicate tread. As if to express her sense that it was good to be alive, young, and healthy in the midst of the finest green grass on a sunny, spring morning, she let out a great whinny that sounded as proud as a trumpet blast.

Almost immediately she was answered by a distant whinny that rang out just as proud.

It was not Hobgoblin who answered her. In his greed he had just licked his silver manger clean to the last grain and had nodded off peacefully to enjoy a small siesta.

It was the voice of El Scham— as much on his toes, as high strung, as fiery as ever—who doubtless heard in Roxana's whinny an echo of the fair, white beauties he used to serve in Tunis.

When she heard him, she halted and looked around inquiringly. Turning her fine head with its enormous eye toward the stud, she seemed to take on an expression of extraordinary and intelligent interest, cocked her ear, and began to listen with the utmost attention.

But nothing was to be heard but the spring breeze rustling the foliage, as

Lord Godolphin and his guests held their breath.

Doubtless disturbed by the continuing silence, Roxana gave a second whinny—shorter, less confident, more inquiring.

Rendered torpid by his food, Hobgoblin slumbered on. It was El Scham who responded, twice making the walls of Gogmagog resound with the most piercing, terrible, passionate call that has ever been heard from a valiant king of the desert.

Roxana heard him like a horse obsessed. She stood there trembling, her breath coming in short gasps. Her flanks heaved and her coat, which had just seemed so pale and smooth, broke out in a feverish sweat that left dark patches here and there. Confused and torn perhaps between the urge to answer El Scham and a natural sense of modesty and decorum, twice she seemed ready to reply to him, and twice she restrained herself at the last minute.

All of a sudden her attention was drawn by a second whinny—heavier, more awkward (muted almost) and entirely too short. It was his lordship Hobgoblin who had finally woken up, heard the other horses, and was now replying to a call that he presumptuously assumed had been intended for him. Words cannot be found to describe the scornful attitude Roxana adopted when she heard his wheezing summons. But when she heard the renewed call of El Scham, which rang out fiercer still, tinged as it now was with a note of angry rivalry—a call of defiance directed at the presumptuous Hobgoblin—she could restrain herself no longer and answered El Scham with a shameless, radiant, imperious call of her own, a call that began softly and plaintively to culminate in tones of raw and unrestrained passion.

Hobgoblin tried his best to join this amorous conversation, but his attempts were met either with Roxana's scornful silence, or with the furious responses of El Scham that quite eclipsed Hobgoblin's short winded and tentative interventions. Lord Godolphin and his guests had been much amused by the exchange, however he observed to Chifney as he led the mare away that "the teaser is already braying like a jackass, which means the poor devil will do his miserable job well enough."

That evening after dinner, as the port was making its way round the polished mahogany table, the assembled company drank numerous toasts to the future union of Hobgoblin and Roxana and to their numerous progeny, upon which Lord Godolphin rested the most extravagant hopes and expectations.

Chapter Eleven

The Wheatear

Some three years had passed since Roxana first engaged the peerless El Scham in amorous conversation. Although it was springtime, the weather was cold and rainy. A blustery west wind was blowing and only the first light of dawn showed where the horizon ended and the dark rainclouds began. In the middle of a blasted heath, totally empty and seemingly without end, there huddled a man, a horse, and a cat. Needless to say the man was Agba, the horse El Scham, and the cat the steadfast, brave-hearted Grimalkin.

Chapter Eleven

The Arab had constructed a kind of byre out of stone and mud, with a roof of ferns. There he sat hunched up and covered with his old camel hair burnous. Grimalkin lay stretched at his feet, feeling pretty wretched, but determined to put a brave face on things. The cold wind blowing over the heath stirred El Scham's mane and tail. He was standing in the lee of the byre, cropping the occasional blades of spring grass that were finally beginning to make their appearance through the growth of heather. The barb's dull, shaggy coat made it obvious that it was a long time since he had seen the inside of a stable.

From time to time, Agba clapped his hands and an obedient El Scham would approach happily, look at him with his gentle, intelligent gaze, and gratefully receive a stroke or two, or a handful of hay. He would then return to the heath, which he would sometimes traverse in a careering liberated gallop, which made him look like a magnificent beast of the wild.

Sometimes, toward sunset, he would pause, looking thoughtful and concerned, standing there sadly with an inquiring air. At such moment, the silhouette of the noble beast with his flowing mane and tail stood out black against the evening sky and seemed to dominate the landscape like a giant apparition.

To what stroke of ill fortune did Agba, El Scham, and Grimalkin owe their disgrace and banishment from Gogmagog Stud and their current wretched circumstance?

Agba had fallen hopelessly in love with Roxana, as if on behalf of El Scham. He suffered all the miseries of intense jealousy when he realized that his horse would have to forget the mare forever, since, notwithstanding her scornful rejection of Hobgoblin and the powerful inclination that she felt toward El Scham,

she was reserved for the Sultan of Gogmagog.

But these pangs of jealousy were as
nothing to Agba's misery when he finally
discovered the use El Scham was to be
put to. The news nearly sent him mad.
Were it not for his faith, for the respect—
nay veneration—in which he held El
Scham, and for the deeply rooted belief
that his horse was destined for eventual
greatness, he would have killed El Scham
and taken his own life, thereby sparing
them both the ultimate degradation.

Even though the stable lads mocked
and jeered at him, Agba swallowed his
shame, concealed his fury, and continued
to put his trust in destiny. He resigned
himself to seeing El Scham fulfill his lu-
dicrous and humiliating function for a
full two months, until the return of Roxana, who had lost condition soon after
her arrival at the stud, but who was now
fully restored. The time had now come

for El Scham, as it were, to pave the way for the imperious Hobgoblin, and Agba thought he would go out of his mind as the fateful day dawned.

Let it be said at the outset that Roxana, who had doubtless recognized El Scham from his whinny, displayed nothing but hostile rejection toward Hobgoblin. Her behavior was a mystery to Lord Godolphin and his friends who had come to observe the union. Roxana treated Sultan Hobgoblin with scornful—indeed brutal—disdain, only responding to the passionate whinnies of the barb, who had been forcibly returned to his loose-box.

Overcome with delight on discovering that she remained faithful to his beloved charge, and at the risk of causing a terrible fight between El Scham and Hobgoblin, Agba, in a fit of madness, opened the door to El Scham's box and set him free.

With one great stride, El Scham floated into the yard, and just the sight of him put Hobgoblin's grooms to flight. Lord Godolphin looked helplessly on, uttering the most dreadful threats and ordering Agba to do what he could to catch his horse before he attacked Hobgoblin.

But Agba, who had suffered so much for so long, was drunk with rage, hope, and admiration. El Scham's time had come at last; at last he could wreak a double revenge on Hobgoblin. Instead of obeying his lordship, he even locked the only door that lead out of the yard to prevent anyone from trying to put a stop to the terrible battle that was about to commence between El Scham and Hobgoblin for the mare Roxana. Tied to a post, she seemed to be egging the Arabian on with her urgent whinnies.

Words cannot describe the heroic battle that now ensued. Surprised, almost startled to discover they were free, the two stallions appeared hesitant at first, examining each other carefully as they made their approaches.

El Scham was almost black, Hobgoblin was a grey, and they were both enraged with jealous fury by the proximity of Roxana. With their eyes aflame, their nostrils flaring, their veins swollen to bursting point, swinging their tails like battle flags, El Scham and Hobgoblin galloped at each other like jousting champions and crashed against one another in the midst of a cloud of dust.

Shaken for a moment and set back on their powerful hocks, they tried to bite each other. Hobgoblin reared up and tried to kick El Scham in the shoulder before crashing down on him and sinking his teeth into his hindquarter. So terrible was the pain that El Scham sunk almost to his knees, threw his head back, and gave a terrible cry of pain. But he recovered and in turn contrived to bite Hobgoblin at the base of his neck to make the blood spurt from a vein.

Maddened by the pain and the taste of blood, the two stallions continued their furious battle, accompanied by cries of rage, muted for the most part, until they opened their mouths wide and the whinnies rang out like war cries. Panting, filthy with dust, the two warriors were soon covered with sweaty foam. But for all their fury, the tide of battle was turning. Hobgoblin, brave as he was, had been living too well for too long to be fighting fit, whereas the high strung El Scham was at the very peak of condition.

After putting up a brave fight, Hobgoblin began to weaken. Twice El Scham's onslaughts had set him back on his hocks. Now, with exhausted, heaving flanks, he no longer had the will or the strength to resist a third onslaught that brought him to his knees. Getting up in a final effort, he took flight, finding an ignominious refuge in El Scham's loose-box.

The conqueror magnanimously declined to pursue his beaten rival. Proud, radiant, triumphant he remained content to stand in the middle of the battleground. Then, with his head held high, with one eye covered by a blood-soaked forelock, he gave a long triumphant victory whinny. He was greeted by an impatient, passionate, breathless answer. It was Roxana, the victor's spoils.

* * *

As for the Arab, he was utterly absorbed by the terrible fight; his emotions—ranging from initial alarm, through excitement, joy, and intoxication, to ecstatic triumph—had rendered him oblivious to the helpless fury of Lord Godolphin as he witnessed the fate of the stallion he had counted on to secure the future of English bloodstock.

But once the heat of the moment had passed, for El Scham and for Agba, the latter understood all too well that he would have to pay a terrible price for setting his stallion free. And the price was terrible indeed. That very same day El Scham, Agba, and Grimalkin were ejected from Gogmagog and sent into exile to a small farm owned by Lord Godolphin some sixty miles away from the stud. The tenant was instructed to provide Agba with bread and a bed of ferns, while El Scham was to be turned out to live off whatever grazing he could find. Fortunately the resourceful Agba had been able to build him his modest shelter.

As for Roxana, she received the kind of treatment reserved for a wellborn young lady who refuses a good marriage prospect to go off with a highwayman.

Cursed and rejected by all and sundry, she was relegated to a distant foaling box in which the unfortunate mare finally gave birth to El Scham's luckless son. The foal provided the mournful mare, who had never forgotten his sire, with some small degree of comfort, while she continued to refuse to have any relations with the Sultan Hobgoblin.

So it was just over two years after Roxana had given birth that we find the three friends living in solitary exile on a blasted heath. It must be said, however, that exile, for all its rigours, did not cause the "criminals" too much distress. Agba, who had never lost faith in destiny, spent his time dreaming of El Scham's future glory. As long as he was not separated from his horse, the bed of ferns and a diet of black bread were no hardship. As for El Scham, delighted to be free of the ignominious and tantalizing labors that had led to his triumph, his moment of happiness, and his subsequent dis-grace, he was not unhappy to live the life of an unfettered wanderer. Grimalkin had no objections to living off the land ei-ther and found plenty of good hunting among the ferns and heather.

So there they were on that particular rainy morning in early spring—Agba dreaming dreams of glory, El Scham grazing, and Grimalkin working on his coat—when all of a sudden Agba started and looked south, thinking he had heard something. As the sounds seemed to grow louder, he put his ear to the ground to hear them more clearly. As he did so, El Scham began to grow excited, pawing the turf and giving a series of whinnies. Soon it was possible to make out the sound of a number of horses galloping to-ward them across the heath, and a few moments later a rider appeared.

To Agba's utter amazement, it was none other than Chifney himself, followed by two mounted servants and a kind of light cart. A terrified El Scham took flight, while Agba was appalled at the thought that Lord Godolphin might have forgiven them and Chifney had come to take the horse back to perform his former duty. Yet he soon noticed that Chifney was anything but his old mocking and sarcastic self. He gave him a civil greeting and immediately started to talk to him in a warm and friendly tone of voice.

"Now then friend," he said giving him a joyful tap on the shoulder. "There's been some changes at Gogmagog, I can tell you, and you'll be pleased to know what they are. The fact is I've come to fetch you all back to the stud."

Chifney took one look at Agba's apprehensive expression and guessed what he was thinking. His answer was to point to the contents of the cart that one of the servants was unloading.

"Don't you worry about a thing, my friend. Your fellow ain't going to be a teaser no more, not him. Take a look at these lovely soft rugs with his lordship's coat of arms on them. Take a look at these lead lines and the white leather halter, soft as silk, and my box of medicines what always travels with me when I go to bring home a really valuable horse."

Casting a curious eye over the various objects as the servants unloaded them and piled them up in the byre, Agba turned from them to Chifney with an inquiring look.

"Don't you know that no one comes with stuff like this to fetch a teaser?" he said.

"His lordship has never told me to take better care of any horse than your barb. And does he deserve it! I only wish we'd known earlier," he added with a shake of his head.

"But let's try to make up for lost time and get back to Gogmagog as soon as we can. Your precious stallion mustn't spend another minute in a place like this."

Agba quickly recovered from his initial shock. Understanding that El Scham's lucky star had triumphed at last, much to Chifney's astonishment, he showed not the slightest sign of delight or even surprise. He simply picked up a halter, clapped his hands, and in a moment or two, El Scham, who had been keeping close to the byre with a wary look in his eye, came up to him and lowered his head in joyful obedience.

Agba immediately slipped the halter on and draped him in the luxurious rugs that Chifney provided. He was moving like an automaton, like a sleepwalker almost, and indeed it really felt as if he were dreaming. Mounting a horse that one of the servants held for him, Agba took hold of El Scham's lead line and set off at the head of the little procession, accompanied by Grimalkin, who bounded onto El Scham's back to take up his habitual position there. An hour later they had put the blasted heath behind them forever.

The time has now come to explain this extraordinary turn of fortune's wheel, which had taken El Scham, Agba, and Grimalkin from their place of exile to allow the stallion finally to fulfill the glorious destiny that the lucky, white mark had always foretold for him.

Chapter Twelve

The Godolphin Arabian

Roxana HAD HAD A foal by El Scham, a colt named Lath. Sharing the disgrace directed at his sire, punished for a transgression that was none of his doing, he was ignored and neglected in his early months, cared for only by his mother who loved him passionately.

Yet as he began to grow, the antipathy that Lord Godolphin and Chifney had first felt toward him began to diminish. For there had never been a colt with so much promise. Bigger and stronger than any of the rest of the crop, he outran them all effortlessly in the yearlings' mad careers over the great pastures of Gogmagog. Roxana always stayed with him as he ran; galloping upsides her son, she would run just fast enough to incite him to keep up but never so fast as to tire or discourage him.

What more is there to say? By the time he turned two it was obvious that he was going to be a wonder horse, whose noble breeding and extraordinary beauty made him stand out head and shoulders above his contemporaries.

Besides, this was a time when the English prejudice against Arab stallions was slowly beginning to dissipate. The descendants of the Darley Arabian, a barb brought to England from Aleppo by a certain Thomas Darley in 1717 at the end of Queen Anne's reign, were beginning to make such a mark on the turf that breeders were coming to recognize the need to go back to the Arab originals in their search for ultimate strength and beauty.

Indeed the Darley Arabian's offspring—among which were wonders such as Flying Childers, "the fleetest horse ever trained at Newmarket or in any other country" (*General Stud Book*, Volume I, 1891), Dart, Skipjack, Daedalus, Aleppo, and Manica—were lengths ahead of their rivals on Newmarket Heath or Epsom Downs.

So as he watched the almost miraculous development of the El Scham colt, Lord Godolphin indeed recalled that his sire, who was probably as finely bred as the Darley Arabian himself, was living a wretched life in exile amidst ferns and heather. But it takes time to get over a deep-rooted prejudice. It took Lath's contemptuous victories over his rivals in two-year-old trials, together with the extraordinary and universal admiration that he commanded, for Lord Godolphin to realize that El Scham was a treasure indeed, the stallion he had long been looking for that was going to renew the breed. Accordingly, one spring morning he dispatched Chifney to find El Scham in his exile and bring him home in glory.

From that moment on Hobgoblin's star began to wane as his progeny was so easily beaten by the young and precocious Lath who was already showing himself to be a worthy descendant of the Kings of the Wind.

Disappointed in Hobgoblin's failures, and losing the high esteem in which he had once held him, Lord Godolphin began by evicting his one-time favourite from his sumptuous palace, relegating him to a loose-box that was rather less luxurious than the one occupied by El Scham when he first arrived at Gogmagog. Even though the barb did not yet occupy the erstwhile residence of the luckless Hobgoblin, it was obvious that he was working his way into his lordship's good graces. While Agba, not so long ago the object of universal ridicule, was now treated with the greatest respect. And even Grimalkin was benefitting from the good fortune that seemed to radiate from El Scham.

To appreciate the full scale of the stallion's triumph, to see him finally fulfill the glorious destiny foretold by the white mark that had been blocked for so long by his unlucky star, to appreciate the full scale of his magnificent achievements, we must move forward in time from 1734 to 1738. That year three of his colts, each of which was possessed of quite extraordinary quality, were entered in three different races on Newmarket Heath.

Lath in the five-year-olds' race.

Cade in the four-year-olds' race.

Regulus in the three-year-olds' race.

Sure as he was that all three of El Scham's offspring would win their race, Lord Godolphin, eccentric as always, wanted their sire to come and witness their victories in style.

And come he did.

Good living, age, rest, and his professional activities had all combined to fill him out magnificently. Sumptuously decked in an Arabian harness, he advanced gravely over the Heath, wearing a purple rug, ridden by Agba who was just as luxuriously attired in his native robes. For safety's sake and in order to restrain any excessive expressions of paternal pride and joy, a groom walked on either side of him, holding a silken lead line attached to his golden bridle.

El Scham's progeny was already so universally famous, and English lovers of the horse so appreciative of his extraordinary contribution to the improvement of their breed, that his arrival on the race course was greeted with loud applause— until, that is, the runners in the first race came under starter's orders and all eyes turned to the course.

Lord Godolphin's expectations were fulfilled.

The three-year-olds raced first, and the race was won by Regulus, son of El Scham.

Then the four-year-olds ran and the race was won by Cade, son of El Scham.

Finally it was the turn of the five-year-olds, and this time it was Lath who finished first, winning his race for the third year in a row.

The applause for El Scham and his progeny grew and grew, swelling to a crescendo. As for the stallion, he accepted the acclamation with a kind of modest dignity as no more than his due, and appeared scarcely to notice the cheering crowds. Agba, however, was in a kind of ecstasy. Almost delirious with joy, he seemed to be hallucinating, seeing a sky studded with white marks as if they were the very stars of heaven, while at the bottom of the entrails of the earth a myriad black wheatears could be seen sinking into dark oblivion like a flight of bats.

When they returned to Gogmagog after the last race, a final triumph awaited El Scham. From that moment on he would inhabit Hobgoblin's palace, and the final mark of his master's respect, love, and admiration could be seen on the marble portico over the palace entrance where magnificent gold lettering spelt out the words:

THE GODOLPHIN ARABIAN

Thus the son-in-law of the Duke of Marlborough, the son of the illustrious Sidney, one time Lord Treasurer of England, had given his own name to El Scham.

As final proof of the fact that justice is not always blind, not only was the luckless Hobgoblin overthrown and cast into disgrace, but he was also doomed to spend the rest of his days serving as teaser to El Scham—or rather to The Godolphin Arabian.

Agba partook of the barb's good fortune and Grimalkin enjoyed the singular honor of featuring prominently in the portrait that Morier painted of the stallion, a portrait that would later be copied by the great George Stubbs. And so, with that good fortune promised by the white mark forever in the ascendant, The Godolphin Arabian continued to triumph and to add illustrious descendants to the noble Eastern dynasty of the Kings of the Wind.

Through his second colt by Roxana, Cade, he established the famous Matchem Line, and his posterity numbers other great horses such as Babraham, Blanche,

Dismal, Bajazet, Tamerlane, Tarquin, Phoenix, Stag, Blossom, Dormouse, Skewball, Sultan, Noble, and Cripple—not to mention the incomparable Gimcrack, "the sweetest little horse there ever was," according to Lady Sarah Bunbury.[1]

It is worth noting that among the stallion's other illustrious descendants was Three Bars, the Thoroughbred that served as one of the foundation stallions of another magnificent breed: the American Quarter Horse. More important still for the development of the Thoroughbred, his son Regulus was the broodmare sire of

---

1. Lady Bunbury's description would apply equally to two other distinguished descendants, Hyperion and Mill Reef. Among the American descendants of the Godolphin Arabian, we find the immortal Man o' War, War Admiral, and the latter's grandson, Mr. Prospector. Anyone who has ever had any dealings with Mr. Prospector or his progeny and entered their stall at their peril, will perhaps recognize some of the problems that Mr. Rogers or Sam Chifney once encountered when trying to deal with their illustrious ancestor, El Scham!

the immortal Eclipse, the most eloquent witness of them all to the splendour of the Arabian. Eclipse, who was never touched by whip or spur; Eclipse, the fastest horse of his age; Eclipse, who once covered four miles in eight minutes carrying twelve stone; Eclipse, who was never beaten and who died in 1789, arguably the greatest racehorse that ever ran.

What more remains to be said? For the rest of his days the barb lived a life every bit as happy, glorious, honoured, and serene as it had once been plunged in misery.

After a long and productive career, The Godolphin Arabian died a peaceful death at the age of twenty-nine in 1753. A solemn ceremony was performed at the gravesite and he was laid to rest under a gateway to the stable. A stone slab was placed over his grave with an appropriate inscription. Grimalkin did not attend the funeral. The moment that his companion died, he vanished and was found dead a few days later.[2] Agba did not outlive his companions by many months. He, too, died a peaceful death and was no doubt reunited with his friends in paradise.

Such then was the extraordinary life of The Godolphin Arabian, the foundation stallion that, together with the Darley Arabian and the Byerly Turk was responsible for the creation of God's greatest gift to mankind, the modern Thoroughbred. Together they represent the root of that mighty tree that has put forth all those countless precious branches that reach down to the present and transmit the priceless sap that originated with the noble Kings of the Wind that once galloped across the sands of Araby.

---

2. It has been suggested by some breeders that, among Grimalkin's other achievements, he was one of the foundation tomcats that helped establish the British shorthair breed, the feline equivalent of the working Thoroughbred.